ESCAPE IN SRI LANKA

DAWN BROOKES

Dawn Brookes
Publishing

Escape

in

Sri Lanka

DAWN BROOKES

OAKWOOD PUBLISHING

This novel is entirely a work of fiction. The names, characters and incidents portrayed are the work of the author's imagination. Any resemblance to actual persons, living or dead is entirely coincidental. Although real life places are depicted in settings, all situations and people related to those places are fictional.

www.dawnbrookespublishing.com
Paperback Edition 2025
Kindle Edition 2025
Paperback ISBN: 978-1-916842-15-1

Cover Design by Dawn Brookes

PROLOGUE

He shoved clothes and documents into a bag, needing to escape Colombo before something terrible happened to him. His hands shook as he stuffed essentials into the small duffel bag, glancing fearfully at the door of his apartment every few seconds. The morning sun cast long shadows through his window, and his reflection in the mirror revealed how terrified he felt.

Two men had threatened him the day before, cornering him in the pharmacy stockroom. The memory made him shudder. One man's words still rang in his ears: “Everyone has a price. Name yours before it’s too late.” He'd refused to steal medicines for them, and the man’s false friendliness vanished.

"Think carefully about your decision. People who don't cooperate tend to have... accidents."

Davi knew they meant it. It was rumoured that two other pharmacists had given in to their demands, helping them steal prescription drugs to be sold on the street. But he couldn't – wouldn't do it. His faith and conscience wouldn't allow him to take part in their criminal enterprise, no matter how much money they offered or what threats they made.

He grabbed his passport and savings from the locked drawer in his bedroom. His hands shook so much he dropped several rupee notes on the floor. As he bent to pick them up, his eyes fell on the framed photo of his parents. They had raised him to be honest and help others. What would they think if he gave in to corruption? No, he was making the right choice, even if it meant leaving everything behind.

There was one person he needed to warn, though. His friend at the hospital should know what was happening. They had worked together for six months, shared lunches, and confided in each other. If anything happened to him, they would surely go after his friend next. His fingers trembled as he scribbled a hasty note. He'd phoned the night before, but he wanted to put something in writing.

'I have to leave town for a while. It's not safe. Be careful who you trust. I'll call when I can.'

Davi looked around his small apartment one last time. Five years of memories were contained within these walls. His pharmacology degree hung proudly near the door. Photos of friends and family lined the shelves. His collection of Buddhist texts sat neatly arranged on the bookcase. Would he ever see any of it again?

A noise in the hallway made him freeze. Loud footsteps approached his door. His heart pounded as he zipped up the bag. There was more than one set of footsteps. Heavy. Determined. He looked wildly for an escape route, but his third-floor apartment offered no easy way out.

Too late. The door burst open with a crash that seemed to shake the entire building. Two men entered, their faces hard and merciless. Davi recognised them immediately – the same men who had threatened him.

"Going somewhere?" the taller one asked with a cruel smile, glancing at the packed bag on the bed. He wore black trousers, a white shirt, and a black tie. A holstered gun at his hip glinted in the light from the window.

"Please," Davi began, backing away. "I'm not going to—"

"To what? Run away? Report us?" The man's face hardened. "We can't take that risk, Mr

Ranasinghe. We have given you every chance to cooperate."

"I won't help you poison people," Davi said, surprised by the steadiness in his voice despite his terror. If these were his last moments, he would face them with dignity. "What you're doing is wrong."

"Wrong?" The man laughed, a bitter sound devoid of humour. "What's wrong is refusing to help people who offer you a good life." He nodded to his companion.

"Come with us." Davi's heart lurched in his chest. Before he could react, rough hands seized his arms from behind, fingers digging into his flesh. He tried to twist away, but another set of hands grabbed him, forcing his wrists into cuffs. The coarse fabric of a sack scraped against his face as they yanked it over his head, cutting off his vision and filling his nostrils with dust. Davi thrashed and kicked, but his attackers were too strong.

Moments later, his shoulder slammed against something metal – a car door – as they manhandled him towards the vehicle. One of them shoved him forward, forcing him to bend. The lip of the boot caught his shin as they pushed him in, making him gasp in pain. The space was tight and cramped, smelling of rubber and oil. The boot slammed shut with a hollow thud that seemed to seal his fate.

As the engine roared to life, Davi's body was bashed from side to side, his mind racing as frantically as his pulse. Where were they taking him? The journey stretched on, minutes bleeding into what felt like hours, while he lay there in the suffocating darkness, helpless to do anything but wait.

The car stopped, and strong hands lifted him out of the boot, forced him to walk forward, and shoved him inside a building. One of the men cursed about a lift not working. Next, they pushed him up around fourteen flights of stairs. Davi heard a few doors opening and closing quickly. People in Colombo minded their own business.

"Please. Let me go. I told you, I won't—"

"Quiet!" One of the men punched him in the side of the head as they forced him on. The next thing he knew, they pushed him inside a room and removed the sack.

Davi saw her terrified face. "Don't," he said.

The gunshot sounded deafening in the small apartment. Pain exploded in Davi's chest as he crumpled to the floor. Darkness crept into the edges of his vision. He whispered a last prayer – not for himself, but for her and those left behind. His last conscious thought was a hope that she would stay safe.

Then darkness took him.

1

Gwen Sumner shielded her eyes from the glare of the sun reflecting on her computer screen. She had worked as the Senior Nurse on board the *Coral Queen* for three years after transferring from her previous Queen Cruises ship to recover from a failed relationship. The hurt from that affair still haunted her, making her wary of relationships to this day.

She lifted her eyes from the computer, surveying the nurses waiting for instructions. Gwen was determined to leave everything in perfect order before taking a long overdue shore leave. The luxurious cruise ship was docked in Colombo, Sri Lanka, for an extended stay over the Christmas season to undergo essential maintenance and repairs.

"Okay," Gwen began, "Bernard has agreed to be

acting manager for the week I'm away. I know you'll give him your full support." Gwen knew the team could manage themselves, but the ship's policy required a hierarchy remain in place at all times. She continued, "Mrs Garland's son and family are taking her ashore this morning, so she will need her injection at 10 o'clock. Bernard, I'm sure you can see to that while Brigitte and Janet do morning surgery."

Bernard smiled in response. "No problem, boss."

"Mr Patel is coming early for a dressing change. That's you, Brigitte," Gwen said.

"Yes, Sarah normally does it, but she's gone ashore for the day. She briefed me before leaving and promised to cover evening surgery when she gets back."

"Good."

Brigitte, Bernard, and Sarah made an experienced nursing team. Gwen only hoped that Bernard would curtail his habit of winding up the French nurse; otherwise, it would fall upon Sarah to keep the peace. Gwen paused, glancing at her screen again before continuing. "Graham has a meeting with Captain Jenson at nine-thirty, so, unless there's an emergency, please send for Janet." Janet Plover had been working as a junior doctor for the past year, and they sometimes referred to her as the baby doc, an affectionate term used by the medical team. She was competent and efficient and well able to deal with most situations, having worked in accident and emergency departments in Wales before joining the ship.

With jobs allocated and invoices up to date, Gwen felt satisfied all was in order.

"Don't worry about us, boss; you enjoy yourself." Bernard grinned as he stood to leave. Gwen liked Bernard, and his experience of trauma and casualties in Manila made him a solid pair of hands, as skilled as most doctors in a crisis.

"Just behave, Bernard."

His eyes shone with enthusiasm, as they always did, but the cheeky glimmer drew a frown from Gwen.

"He won't," said Brigitte, "but don't worry; we can handle it."

Gwen believed her. When the going got tough, the team pulled together, a reassuring thought. "Have an enjoyable week, then."

"Good morning, Gwen." Dr Graham Bentley, the chief medical officer, entered her office as the others were on their way out. He strode in, eyes sparkling. "I'm glad I caught you. I wanted to check in before my meeting."

Gwen turned to face him. Six feet tall, in his late fifties with short fair hair and greying sideburns,

Graham looked younger than his age, despite the demands of his job and a slight paunch. He wore the crisp white uniform with the number of gold stripes on his epaulettes signalling his senior rank. Forcing herself to look away from his deep brown eyes, she replied, "That's good of you."

"Not at all," Graham said, rubbing his freshly shaved chin thoughtfully. "You know we've got extra supplies coming aboard during our extended stay, but I'm hoping to put it to the senior team that we need more staff. I can't promise we'll get any, at least not permanently."

Gwen had been hoping for some time that they might employ an extra nurse or a healthcare assistant. The team often seemed overstretched these days as more patients with long-term conditions took cruises, but Graham had petitioned for an extra doctor. She hoped it wouldn't be an either/or situation. She could discuss it if Graham secured extra funding. They made these decisions together.

"Another reason I'm here," Graham added, "is that I've been in touch with an old friend from medical school. Ranil Fernando is a consultant physician at the National Hospital, and he's keen to meet for a catch-up. I wondered if you might like to join us?"

Gwen wondered if Graham had forgotten she was

about to take shore leave. "I could try," she said, "although I'll be staying with my cousin Tiffany this coming week and exploring the local culture. I'm looking forward to spending some time on terra firma."

"Of course you are. Sorry I forgot," Graham replied. "I hope you enjoy your leave. You deserve a break. But if you have the time and are happy to, I could arrange to meet Ranil with you and your cousin. We could even meet for lunch or dinner one day."

"That's a possibility. Tiff's a nurse at the same hospital. I'm sure she won't mind as long as your friend isn't the hospital ogre." Gwen grinned. "When I see her, I'll mention it."

"Excellent. I doubt Ranil will be an ogre. If memory serves me right, he was always a soft touch," Graham said, chuckling. "I've got a bit of time before meeting Peter. How about a coffee?" Graham headed towards the coffee machine that was a staple in the office where the team shared downtime and debriefs. He began pouring the freshly brewed liquid into a mug.

"Why not," she said. Graham only referred to Captain Jenson as Peter when with senior officers like herself.

Gwen's fingers hovered over her computer, about

to power it down, when she heard a call from outside the open door. "Excuse me, Sister Sumner?" Gwen crossed the room to find a portly elderly man with a sheen of sweat on his brow clutching his abdomen.

"Mr Thompson!" Gwen recalled his name from a previous visit to the surgery, and thanks to her memory for numbers, she remembered Benjamin Thompson's age, eighty-three. "How can I help you?"

"Terrible pain, Sister," he gasped, eyes scrunched, and perspiration forming on his forehead. "In my stomach."

Gwen's heart rate increased on seeing the pallor cross Mr Thompson's face. "Let's take a look." She guided him to a nearby seat and pressed gently on his abdomen. He groaned in pain.

"Dr Bentley," she called over her shoulder, "would you mind having a look at Mr Thompson?"

"Of course," Graham joined her at the passenger's side. Together, they assisted him into a wheelchair, and Gwen pushed it into the nearest treatment room. His pain seemed to be increasing, and Gwen worried he might not be able to stand.

"We need to get you onto an examination table," she explained.

Through gritted teeth, he assured them he could manage if they helped. Taking an arm each, they assisted him onto the examination table, the paper covering crackling beneath his weight. Once Mr Thompson lay down, Graham carried out a thorough examination. Gwen watched, as she had many times before, how his expert hands palpated the patient's abdomen. "Any nausea or vomiting, Mr Thompson?" Graham asked as he continued palpating.

"None, but the pain's pretty bad, doctor," Mr Thompson groaned, his face growing paler by the second.

"Appendicitis?" Gwen queried, noting Mr Thompson's grimace when Graham palpated over the right iliac fossa.

"More than likely," he concurred, the lines on his forehead deepening. "I'm afraid we need to get you stabilised and transferred to hospital," he said to Mr Thompson.

"I'll call ahead," Gwen said, springing into action. She returned to her office and called for an ambulance to meet them on the port side. Next, she called Raggie, the team's dedicated steward, to bring a stretcher from the storeroom. Afterwards, she put a call through to the National Hospital and spoke to the surgeon on duty before contacting Mr Thompson's daughter to update her on the unfolding situation.

On the way back to the treatment room, Raggie joined her, wheeling a trolley, and Graham informed her that he had administered analgesia and inserted an intravenous cannula into the patient's arm.

"Thank you all," Mr Thompson managed to say.

"Our pleasure, Mr Thompson," Gwen replied, her tone gentle. "Now try to relax while we get you sorted."

Working with practiced efficiency, Gwen and Raggie pushed the stretcher while Graham monitored the patient and the drip. The ambulance pulled up on the port side as they wheeled him down a ramp onto the tarmac. Graham passed his handwritten notes to the Sri Lankan ambulance crew, also giving them a verbal handover. "I'll email the patient's details to the surgical team."

"Hopefully, I'll see you in a few days," said Mr Thompson, giving a shaky wave.

"We'll arrange for some of your belongings to follow you to the hospital," promised Gwen. Mr Thompson was aboard for a world cruise with his daughter and her family. Gwen hoped he could rejoin the ship before it left port. He would be in expert hands in a large city hospital.

As they strolled back up the ramp onto the ship, Gwen caught her breath.

"Thank heavens we're in port," said Graham. "Or I might have been operating on a burst appendix." The gravity of the near miss sank in as they turned to watch the ambulance exit the port gates.

"Times like these remind me of the fragility of chance in our roles," Gwen said.

"You're right," Graham replied, his eyes locked on hers, as if about to say something; then he hesitated.

"Well... It's time I finished up in the office before leaving," Gwen said.

"I'm pleased you joined the *Coral Queen*, Gwen," Graham said, giving her a small smile. "It would be hard to manage these emergencies without your help... and we've experienced our fair share."

Gwen didn't quite know how to react. Graham rarely said things like this. "We might not resolve every emergency, but we do the best we can with the resources at our disposal. I often say that with state-of-the-art equipment and a great team, we have one of the best medical teams sailing the high seas."

"True enough," said Graham, rubbing his chin.

Graham was an asset to the ship, and she had grown fond of him during their time working together... more than fond if she allowed herself to be honest, but she didn't wish to go down that road again. She shook the thought from her mind.

The medical team handled the health of over 5,000 people at any one time under Graham's leadership. He had shared in the past that this sometimes weighed heavily. Once aboard, Graham left Gwen to attend his meeting.

Gwen found a middle-aged woman pacing the floor outside the medical centre, wringing her hands, her face etched with worry.

"Mrs Thompson-Smith?" Gwen asked, stepping forward and resting a comforting hand on her shoulder.

"Y-yes," the woman stammered, her voice trembling. "Is my father going to be all right?"

"He's in excellent hands. The ambulance crew have taken him to the National Hospital. It's the biggest and best in Colombo. As I mentioned on the phone, Dr Bentley believes he has appendicitis. I expect he'll need belongings for a few days."

"At least they'll be able to treat him. Thank you," Mrs Thompson-Smith said, tears welling in her eyes. "I just don't know what I'd do without him."

"Try not to worry," Gwen said soothingly, knowing she was asking for the impossible when there were always risks associated with surgery. "Your father is strong and otherwise in good health. The hospital has an excellent reputation."

Mrs Thompson-Smith nodded. "I'll pack a bag and take a taxi. My husband's trying to find his insurance documents."

"No need for that. I'll contact the insurance

company with the details. You just concentrate on your father and leave the administration side of things to us." Gwen allowed herself a small smile. Moments when she could provide a little comfort to those in need made her job worthwhile.

After Mrs Thompson-Smith left, Gwen returned to her office and completed the administration for Mr Thompson's admission. She informed Bernard of the admission and asked him to keep in contact with the hospital and Mrs Thompson-Smith. Once satisfied that everything was in order, Gwen went to her room to retrieve her suitcase.

Forty minutes later, she headed for the exit and felt a slight quickening of her heart rate when she saw Graham waiting near the security desks as passengers lined up to go ashore.

He smiled when he saw her. "I just wanted to let you know Captain Jenson has agreed to some extra supplies being delivered."

"Anything about extra staff?"

"It wasn't the right time to mention it," he said, lowering his voice. "The spare parts are going to cost a fortune."

"Oh well, we can't have everything," she said, feeling slightly awkward.

"Safe journey."

"Thanks. I'll see you soon. Let me know if there are any emergencies and I'll come rushing back."

"No way. You are going to enjoy your break. If I arrange anything with Ranil, I'll call you," Graham said, his eyes scanning the horizon. "If it's convenient, that is. I wouldn't want to spoil your plans."

"It won't spoil our plans. I don't even know what we're doing yet," Gwen replied.

"Is your cousin Tiffany on leave?" Graham asked, running a hand through his hair.

"She said she'd try to get a few days off, so fingers crossed she is." Gwen hoped so. She had been to Colombo before but had only ever managed a few hours of snatched shore leave. It would be great to explore the city in depth.

"The architecture and food in Sri Lanka are remarkable. I'm almost envious." Graham's voice pulled her from her musings.

"I know there's a lot of history here – ancient temples, old colonial buildings. I'm looking forward to being a tourist."

"Be sure to take plenty of photographs," Graham said.

"I will," she replied, grinning. "I'll regale you with tales of my escapades over cups of coffee. But hopefully, I'll see you ashore with your old mate."

Graham raised an eyebrow. "You can take the girl

out of Australia, but you can't take Australia out of the girl." They stood in awkward silence before Graham cleared his throat. "Well, I'd best get back to work. Speak soon."

"See ya," Gwen called, over-exaggerating her Australian accent. As she watched him go, a strange sense of unease settled in the pit of her stomach. Gwen shook her head, dismissing the feeling as nothing more than pre-holiday jitters.

With one last glance at her retreating friend, for friend he was, Gwen turned and headed to the security exit.

2

Uncertain, how busy the capital city's roads might be, Gwen arrived at the Taj Samudra Hotel half an hour early. The sights and sounds of the densely populated metropolis overwhelmed her senses during the taxi ride and lingered even after she entered the hotel.

As Gwen stepped into the grand lobby, she was immediately struck by its soaring ceiling and elegant marble floors. The space felt open, with large windows offering panoramic views of the Indian Ocean and the surrounding cityscape. Intricate wooden carvings and traditional artwork blended colonial elegance with modern luxury.

The lobby radiated sophistication. Polished brass accents gleamed softly, while plush seating areas with rich, deep-toned upholstery provided pockets of comfort for guests sipping drinks and chatting. The air conditioning created a pleasant coolness, and she caught a whiff of fresh flowers as she approached the reception desk.

Overhead, a stunning chandelier drew her attention. The hotel's large windows allowed natural light to stream in, creating a bright, airy atmosphere that contrasted with the bustling energy of Colombo just outside.

Despite the busy reception area, it appeared calm and efficient. Well-dressed staff attended to guests with friendly smiles. When her turn came, a young woman with light brown eyes greeted her. "Welcome to the Taj Samudra, Madam. How may I assist you?"

"I'm not checking in, sadly, although the place looks amazing. I'm meeting a cousin for lunch. She works in Colombo. Is there anywhere I can leave my suitcase?"

"Yes, of course, Madam. I'll store it in the baggage area for you." The woman handed her half of a ticket docket and moved around to attach the other half to Gwen's case. "There. Enjoy your lunch."

"Thanks," Gwen replied, heading into the restaurant with a flutter of excited anticipation in her chest.

Gwen checked her watch for the fifth time, craning her neck to peer around people enjoying their meals in the restaurant. She had been expecting Tiffany to arrive at any moment for the past hour. Sipping the last dregs of lukewarm coffee, Gwen tried to suppress the growing anxiety in her stomach as she scanned the crowded room for a glimpse of her cousin. The clinking of cutlery and the murmur of conversations filled the air, but Gwen found it increasingly difficult to relax. Her eyes flitted from table to table, searching for any sign of Tiffany in case she had missed her arrival.

"Excuse me, ma'am." Gwen turned to see the waiter, who had introduced himself as Darsh when she'd ordered her drink, hovering nearby. Looking up at the tall man with dark brown skin and cropped black hair, she noticed his brow was furrowed and his brown eyes narrowed as he looked at her. "Is there something else I can get you? Lunch, perhaps?" There was a hint of impatience in his tone. Gwen had occupied the table in the busy restaurant longer than intended, having only ordered a pot of coffee.

Darsh's eyes flicked between her and a stern-looking man glaring at them. "I'm sorry, Darsh. I'm waiting for someone... my cousin. She must be running late."

"It's busy today, and Colombo traffic can be unpredictable at the best of times, ma'am. With Christmas coming... well..." He shrugged.

"Is there somewhere else I could wait for her?"

Darsh mopped his brow, trying to hide his relief. "Of course, ma'am. The lobby in the main reception is just outside the restaurant. Or, if you go down the corridor and off to the left, there's a bar."

Gwen exhaled heavily. "I came in that way. I've left my case in reception." Words were spilling out of her mouth, but her thoughts were elsewhere. Something must have happened to Tiffany. She hoped her cousin hadn't been involved in an accident. They had hastily arranged the meeting when Gwen learned that the ship would be staying longer in Colombo while awaiting repairs.

Passengers sailing on a world cruise were being compensated for the delay with extra onboard spending money. As the stopover could last a couple of weeks, some opted to move into hotels like this one for Christmas. The ship's departure depended on parts being delivered from India.

When Gwen called Tiffany, her cousin had been ecstatic at the prospect of hosting her during her leave. So why wasn't she here?

Darsh cleared his throat, obviously waiting for her to move.

"If a Tiffany Lee arrives and asks for Gwen Sumner, please let her know where I am? She's Australian like me, a few inches shorter, with long blonde hair." Gwen hadn't seen Tiffany for almost five years, but they kept in touch via social media. "She might be wearing a uniform – she works as a nurse at the National Hospital."

"Very good, ma'am. Tiffany, you say? A nurse?" Was there a flicker of concern in the waiter's eyes?

"Yes. Do you know her?"

Darsh avoided eye contact. "No, ma'am, but if someone by that name appears, I'll be sure to let her know where you are." A glimmer of sweat appeared above the neatly trimmed black moustache of the agitated waiter.

"Are you sure you don't know her?"

Darsh straightened his waistcoat. "Sorry, ma'am... No. I thought I recognised the name, but I don't..."

"Waiter?" A burly man with an impatient tone called from the next table. "We're ready to order."

"Excuse me." Darsh left her to push her chair away as he hurried off.

Gwen rubbed her head as she exited the restaurant. "Strange man."

Rather than sitting in the lobby, Gwen held a mini

conference with herself. She didn't see the point in waiting at the hotel any longer. Her cousin hadn't responded to phone calls or texts, but Gwen had her address. The Tiffany Gwen knew always arrived on time, and if she was delayed, she would have called.

Why haven't you called, Tiff? Gwen tried phoning again, but the call went straight to voicemail. "Hi, Tiffany Lee here..." The familiar Australian drawl made Gwen feel homesick. "...leave a message and I'll get back to you."

"Hi, Tiff, it's Gwen again. You've obviously been delayed. I hope you haven't forgotten I'm arriving today," Gwen said, laughing nervously. "I'm about to leave the hotel and head over to your place."

She strolled back to the reception desk, where the friendly woman with the bright smile and attentive eyes was dealing with guests checking in. Once she finished with them and directed a bellboy to take their bags, she flashed Gwen a smile. "Back already? I thought you'd be hours. Our lunches are renowned."

"I didn't get the pleasure. My cousin didn't show. She's a nurse at the hospital; maybe she got called in to work."

"Would you like me to check with the hospital? Is it the National?"

"Yes, but there's no need to bother them. I'll go to her place and wait." Gwen took an address book out of her handbag. "Can you tell me where this place is?"

"Yes," the receptionist said, examining the address. "It's a short taxi ride from the hotel. If you like, I can arrange for a taxi."

Gwen glanced around the lobby, noting the bustling hotel guests and the air of luxury that surrounded it. "Thank you, that would be great."

The receptionist retrieved Gwen's suitcase and led her outside via the revolving door at the hotel entrance, where she spoke to the concierge in what Gwen assumed was Sinhalese. Her guidebook informed her that the languages of the country included Sinhalese as the most widely spoken, followed by English and Tamil. The concierge waved a taxi forward.

"I hope you find your cousin. Enjoy your stay in Sri Lanka."

"Thanks again," Gwen said. The receptionist returned to the hotel. The outside air felt hot and dry, perfect for the holiday she had been hoping for. Gwen waited while the driver placed her suitcase in the boot of his car.

3

Gwen was about to climb into the taxi when she jumped at the feel of a hand on her shoulder. Seeing the waiter from the restaurant surprised her. "Darsh? Did I forget something?"

"No, Ma'am Sumner, may I have a word?" he spoke in a hushed tone, glancing around.

"Of course," Gwen replied. "Is it about Tiffany?"

"I shouldn't be saying this... I couldn't speak inside, but something's not right."

Gwen's heart raced as she studied the worried expression on Darsh's face. "What do you mean? Is Tiffany in some kind of trouble?"

"Sorry, I know nothing about your cousin's whereabouts, but she often comes to the hotel with a friend of mine," said Darsh. "It might be nothing, but my friend, Davi Ranasinghe, is a pharmacist at the same hospital as your cousin – and he's been acting strangely lately."

"Strangely how?" Gwen's mind raced with potential scenarios.

"I can't say for certain, but I have the impression he's scared of something or someone," he said, his eyes darting back to the hotel. "It might be nothing, but I thought you should know."

Gwen wasn't sure how helpful the information was. All it did was send her anxiety levels through the roof. "I'd better be going," she said.

"Be careful," Darsh warned. "Colombo is a beautiful city, but it can be dangerous if you mix with the wrong people."

Is that what he was hinting at? Had Tiffany and her friend Davi got mixed up with the wrong people? Gwen climbed into the taxi, her heart pounding in her chest. She was still trying to find a seatbelt when the taxi sped away from the hotel. The cityscape blurred past, but she wasn't taking it in. The taxi driver appeared to have a death wish as he flew through busy traffic, blasting his horn and swerving through spaces barely able to accommodate his car. Gwen had travelled the world enough times to realise this style of driving was not uncommon in Asia and Latin America, but she never got used to it. The journey ended with the taxi screeching to a halt outside a new-looking high-rise condo development. Prising her white knuckles from the seat, Gwen opened the door and stepped onto the pavement. She waited while the driver removed her suitcase from the boot.

"Nice place your friend has," he said.

"Yeah, it looks that way." She unzipped her money belt and paid the fare they had settled upon.

"Enjoy your stay in Sri Lanka, but be cautious. Don't go out on your own at night and ignore men who offer you drugs."

"Thanks for the advice. My cousin lives here; she'll keep me on the right path."

"Good." The driver jumped back inside his taxi and sped off into busy traffic without indicating.

Gwen muttered to herself, still amazed that the seatbelts in the taxi weren't working. "He's going to get himself or one of his passengers killed." She pulled the small address book from her belt, found the number, and pressed the buzzer. There was no reply, but an elderly man heading out opened the door, not batting an eyelid as she took the handle and entered with her suitcase in tow. Gwen hoped Tiffany had somehow mixed up her arrival date and would be pleased to see her. Although the building appeared to be relatively new, graffiti lined the outside walls. Inside was cleaner. Gwen approached the lifts and pressed a button.

A man appeared via the stairs and spoke to her in Sinhalese. She didn't understand what he was trying to say until he pointed at the lift, holding his hands out and making an X sign with his forefingers. She nodded. "The lift's broken. Is there another one?"

The man ranted, waving his arms around, presumably about the state of the lifts. She showed him her address book and pointed to Tiffany's. He donned glasses to inspect it, then nodded, saying something while pointing to the stairs where he had come from.

"Which floor?" she asked as he handed back the book.

He shook his head, so she tried signing, using her fingers to count. The man got it and let her count to ten before motioning for her to continue. He stopped her when she got to fourteen.

Her heart sank as her eyes widened. "Fourteenth? You've got to be kidding me."

The man shrugged and wandered out onto the street, muttering something else in Sinhalese, probably relating to silly foreigners.

Gwen looked at her suitcase, wishing she'd left it at the hotel. "Don't they have concierges in these places?" She tried calling Tiffany again, but just like before, it went straight to answerphone.

"Hello, you've got through to Tiffany Lee etc."

"Tiff, it's Gwen again. I'm at your condo. If you're not home, I'll wait outside your flat. How long's the lift been out, by the way? Plus, why the fourteenth floor?" Gwen forced a laugh. "See you upstairs."

Gwen stood at the foot of the stairs, wondering how in the world she was going to haul her case up so many floors when she spotted a porter trolley in the lobby's corner. She moved to the side of the desk, where she presumed a concierge should be, and knocked on the door. A young man came out, probably in his mid-to-late twenties; handsome in a dark, brooding way. He removed his glasses before smiling, revealing exceptionally white teeth.

"You are staying here?" His voice was deep and velvety.

"I'm Gwen Sumner, Tiffany Lee's cousin." She showed him the page in her address book.

The man moved closer and read with his head tilted. "Tiffany?"

"Yes, is she in?"

"Maybe," he said, moving his head from side to side.

"Can I leave my case here while I go up?"

"Sure," he said, placing it on the trolley before

turning back through the door, where she heard a television programme with loud music.

Gwen gazed at the lone suitcase perched on the trolley in the expansive lobby. A knot of anxiety twisted in her stomach. Leaving it unattended was not an option. Resigned, she steeled herself for the inevitable exertion and took possession of it.

The case seemed to have doubled in weight; every item of clothing, every piece of jewellery she had packed, a tangible reminder of the effort required to draw it upwards. The muscles in her arms strained, her grip slipping slightly on the handle as she wrestled with the case.

Reaching the first landing felt like a small victory won through sweat and exertion. She allowed herself a brief respite, opening and closing her hands in preparation for the next flight.

The echo of the case being dragged against the uncarpeted stairs shattered the silence as Gwen resumed her uphill battle. Each thud seemed in time with her racing heart. By the time she conquered the fifth floor, she was blowing hard. She released the handle, her muscles trembling from the effort. Panting, she leaned against the wall to catch her breath.

Barely able to stand, she slumped against the wall, willing her heart rate to slow when footsteps from above made her look up. Her eyes met those of a young man peering over the banister from the sixth floor. Gwen raised a hand, unsure what to do next.

The young man's friendly face broke into a warm smile as he beckoned her up. Gwen sighed, relief easing the tension in her shoulders.

"I need to get to the fourteenth floor," she explained, hoping he understood English.

"No problem, auntie." He took the handle of her case and carried it up the remaining eight flights with ease.

She was breathless when she finally caught up with him. "Thank you so much. It might have taken me all day without your help."

He tilted his head from side to side, just like the other man had done. "Welcome, auntie," he said and ran back down the stairs.

Gwen sat on her suitcase for a few minutes' respite. Once she had recovered enough to walk, she checked her address book for the flat number she was looking for once more and wheeled the case along the poorly lit, vinyl-floored corridor to number 1436.

Arriving at the correct apartment, she felt relieved to see the door ajar. On knocking, it swung open. Gwen gasped. Her hand flew to her mouth.

4

Gwen's knees felt weak as she took hesitant steps toward a man lying on the floor. His blue shirt was stained red, a bullet hole in his chest. Her cousin sat in a corner, hugging her knees drawn up to her face, a strange whimpering sound escaping her mouth. Gwen's nursing instinct kicked in as she knelt down to touch the young man's neck with trembling fingers. No pulse. She moved her eyes away from the body to Tiffany.

"Tiff..." Gwen rushed across the room to her cousin, relieved she was alive. She lifted Tiffany's chin, brushing back damp blonde strands of hair in the hope of forcing her to open her swollen eyelids. "Tiff. It's me. What happened here? Have you called the police?"

Tiffany opened her swollen eyelids, her eyes staring at Gwen as if coming out of a trance. Her voice quivered as she spoke. “They shot him.” Tears welled in her cat-green eyes, and she started shaking.

“Who is he, Tiff, and who shot him?”

Gwen squeezed her cousin's arm. Tiffany whimpered in shock. Gwen tried to process the situation she had walked into. Realising Tiffany was in no state to speak, she approached the victim again, crouching down. She checked his pocket for ID, her hands shaking. Nothing. The mixture of aftershave and dried blood filled her nostrils. The red staining was worse around a single hole in his shirt. It looked as though he’d been executed, and from what little Tiffany had said, it sounded like it too.

She returned to sit down next to Tiffany. “Why aren’t the police here?” No answer.

“I’ve been trying to call you. When did this happen?” There were so many unanswered questions.

Tiffany whimpered again. “The men told me not to call the police. A couple of hours ago... maybe more.” Tears dripped onto her orange t-shirt.

Gwen touched her shoulder. “Tiffany. You need to look at me and tell me exactly what happened.”

“I was getting ready to meet you. Two men burst in; they pushed Davi inside. They had guns.”

Davi, that was the name of the pharmacist Darsh

had mentioned. "Who were these men? Did you recognise them?"

"I've seen one of them before, mooching around the hospital. He could work there. I don't know."

"How did they get in?"

"The door was unlocked. They shoved Davi in. He looked terrified. Before I knew what was happening, they just shot him. Right there." Tiffany pointed to the body before lowering her head into her hands. The air filled with the sound of sobbing.

"Whatever these men said, Tiff, we have to call the police," said Gwen.

Tiffany's eyes widened. Terror filled them. "I'm telling you. They warned me not to go to the police." The words spilled between broken breaths. "They told me they'd be in touch, and the man who shot Davi told me if I went to the police, it would be me next."

Gwen's mind raced. She pulled Tiffany into a hug. "You must know something. Why bring him here? What do these men want from you?"

"I'm thinking Davi refused to give them drugs; he works... worked in the pharmacy. The hospital has had an issue with drug theft." She gulped air into her lungs before adding, "It's gonna be me next, Gwen, because I can't give them what they want."

Gwen wondered if this was why Darsh had

mentioned Davi behaving strangely and being frightened. A drug gang's involvement would explain that, as well as the execution-style killing. With tension rising in her chest and her heart feeling like it might explode, she gripped Tiffany's arms. "We don't have any choice, Tiff. We have to call the police, and we have to do it now."

"Please, Gwen." The cracked voice of her usually capable cousin almost broke Gwen. Her stomach churned. "I'm sorry for not meeting you or answering the phone, but I'm terrified."

"I understand," said Gwen, softening her tone.

"What am I supposed to do?"

Gwen got up, putting her hands out for Tiffany to hold. She pulled her from the floor and guided her through a door that led into her bedroom. They sat on the edge of a divan where Gwen put an arm around her younger cousin's shoulder. "We can't leave a man's body lying in your lounge and do nothing about it."

"The men said they would come back for him later." Tiffany's voice was barely a whisper as her eyes darted to the door, as if the men might turn up at any moment.

"Then we mustn't waste any more time. We need to act before they do." Gwen took her phone from her handbag.

"No, Gwen. Please... I'll come with you to the police station, but I don't want to stay here in case they find us."

"Fine. Let's go. The sooner we get this over with, the better."

Tiffany moved in slow motion, still dazed. After they sidled past the body, Tiffany locked the door at Gwen's insistence. Gwen didn't want to leave her case behind, feeling it would be better if the men didn't know someone else was aware of their crime. Reluctantly, she lugged it down fifteen flights to the basement exit, following Tiffany into a dimly lit car park. A few nods and greetings from elderly residents on the stairs brought a forced grimace-like smile to Tiffany's face. The best effort Gwen had seen.

Tiffany's hands were still trembling when she unlocked the boot of a battered old Mini, but Gwen's case wouldn't fit inside, so they squeezed it into the back seat. Gwen was too tall for the car but resigned herself to the discomfort for the task at hand. The car was just the right size for her cousin, who stood around five inches shorter than Gwen.

"Are you going to be okay to drive?" Gwen asked, concerned.

Tiffany swallowed hard before nodding.

During a twenty-minute drive through hazy roads packed with heavy traffic, there were a few hair-raising moments when tuk-tuks pulled out in front of them without warning. Gwen was already running on adrenaline, and the journey wasn't helping.

"Sorry," Tiffany said as she slammed on the brakes to avoid hitting the back of a car stopped at traffic lights. Her knuckles gripped the steering wheel as if holding on for dear life.

Gwen kept pressing on the imaginary brake pedal in the passenger seat, unable to stop herself.

"I've been driving in Sri Lanka for a little while now, and it's always like this; I usually know how to handle the traffic."

Despite the erratic driving, her cousin sounded more like herself. The drive was proving to be a worthwhile distraction from the trauma she had experienced. "Yes, but do the other drivers know how to handle you?"

Tiffany forced a grin, eventually pulling the car up on a main road. Gwen recognised the police station sign ahead of them. Much of the dual signage in Colombo featured English dating back to when Ceylon was a British colony until 1948. Pleased to have arrived at their destination, she took a deep breath, although she wasn't able to slow down her heart rate. This wasn't the day she had been expecting.

Tiffany released the steering wheel, visibly relaxing.

They sat for a few moments, each gathering their thoughts. A blue Suzuki Alto pulled in three cars ahead of them. Gwen opened the passenger door, and two men emerged from the Suzuki. Tiffany froze. She was staring at a tall man wearing black trousers, a white shirt, and a loosely knotted black tie. He was carrying his jacket over his shoulder. The holstered handgun suggested he was a plain-clothes detective.

“We have to do this, Tiff. Come on.”

5

Tiffany remained frozen to the spot, her eyes wide like saucers. She was trembling. "Shut the door," she snapped.

Gwen opened her mouth to protest, but Tiffany's gasp made her stop.

"That's him. The tall man with the gun. He's one of the men who came to my flat. The man who shot Davi. We can't go in there."

Gwen did as instructed, feeling her stomach knot. They watched as a police officer in uniform stood to attention when the two men approached.

"Are you sure it's the same man who killed your friend?"

"I'll never forget his face, Gwen."

"What about the other one?"

"He wasn't there."

This situation couldn't get any worse. The murderer was a police detective. It took a few minutes for the realisation to sink in. They hid their faces when the men looked down the road while speaking briefly to another uniformed officer.

As soon as the detectives moved inside, Tiffany started the car and executed a one-eighty turn. They were hidden in traffic within seconds, following the route back to Tiffany's condo. Tiffany was shaking and barely able to catch her breath when they returned to the car park. "Cup your hands against your face and breathe in and out," Gwen instructed.

Once Tiffany's panic attack subsided, they took a slow trek upstairs. Gwen tried to think of solutions. They couldn't stay at the condo because the men had told Tiffany they were coming back for the body. She took slow, deep breaths to prevent herself from spiralling out of control. It was vital she held it together. Gwen suggested they go into the kitchen, where Tiffany flopped onto a chair, her head in her hands. Pouring her a drink of water, Gwen collected a blanket from her cousin's bedroom and covered the body.

Then she rummaged through her handbag and found a small packet of tissues, which she handed to Tiffany, who was crying again.

"Gwen, I'm so sorry." Tiffany gasped between sobs.

"You have no need to be sorry, Tiff. None of this is your fault. And I understand we can't go to the police in Colombo. Maybe we can think of something else." Gwen racked her brains.

Tiffany stopped crying, trying to take deep breaths. "I don't know what to do."

"Let's just take a minute, okay? I need to think. One thing's for sure: we can't stay here." Gwen forced herself to focus on the problem as though it were a medical emergency. "Right, I suggest you write down everything that happened here today, including descriptions of the murderer and his accomplice. After that, you need to pack a bag. We'll go to a hotel and figure it out from there."

"What about Davi? I can't just leave him."

"You have to, Tiff. If we call the authorities now, that detective will make sure they suspect you did this. Do as I say. Please."

While Tiffany scribbled her recollections on a notepad, Gwen kept watch on the street outside. Although she felt certain the detective wouldn't come back in daylight to remove a body, there was an element of doubt. He might not do the deed himself, so she was taking no chances. Numerous people left the building, but nobody entered. Traffic moved at the reckless rate she had thus far experienced, but none parked outside. Gwen's brain felt as if it had been hot-wired into the mains electricity. Had it been a computer, it would be overheating. After Tiffany finished writing, she handed the sheet of paper to Gwen, who folded it and placed it in her handbag.

"Gwen, I'm so scared."

"Me too," said Gwen, meaning it. It wasn't every day one walked into a room and found a man shot to death. "Get packed, and we'll find somewhere safe to go."

Tiffany stared at Gwen, a mix of fear and admiration in her eyes. "How do you always know what to do?"

"I don't," Gwen answered with a grim smile, swallowing hard. She would need to summon ideas from somewhere if her cousin was going to survive this ordeal. She continued racking her brain while Tiffany packed. By the time her cousin came out of her bedroom with a small case, Gwen had the crumbs of a plan.

Tiffany's voice sounded hoarse as she spoke. "Gwen, there's something I forgot to mention."

"Tell me."

"Davi phoned me yesterday." Her eyes filled with tears. "He told me he had to leave town for a while.

He wouldn't say why, but now this has happened... it makes sense."

"Did he mention anyone by name or hint at why these men might target him?"

"Not yesterday," Tiffany said, shaking her head. "But he told me before that some pharmacists were being bought off by drug gangs. I tried to persuade him to tell me what was going on, but he wouldn't say anything else. I have no proof he refused to sell them drugs, but now we know one of them is a cop; they could say he was on the take, and that I'm involved."

Gwen knew this was true but didn't want to contemplate it for now. "It's risky for them to do that, and right now we are a step ahead of them. We need to keep it that way."

"Where will we go?"

"We'll start with a big hotel. We can't rely on the police for protection, but I've got an idea of someone who may help."

"Who?" Tiffany asked, her eyes wide with fear. "Anyone I know could be compromised or in danger."

Gwen pursed her lips, considering the option. "I need coffee first. It's time to leave."

Tiffany walked over to her friend and pulled back the blanket. She kissed his forehead. "I'm so sorry, Davi." She looked as if she might crumple, so Gwen took her arm. Encouraging her out of the condo,

Gwen took the handle of her cousin's luggage in the other hand. This time it was Tiffany's suitcase making the journey. Tiffany locked the door, and they made the trek downstairs in silence. Thankfully, when they got to the car, Tiffany's suitcase was smaller than Gwen's and fitted in the boot.

"Where to?" Her cousin climbed into the driver's seat.

"Is there another big hotel besides the Taj Samudra? I don't want to run into the waiter there because he said he knew Davi."

"You met Darsh?"

"Yes. Do you know him?"

"No, but Davi did; we often went to that hotel for meals," said Tiffany. "There's a Hilton; we never went there."

"Then that's the place to start. Did you pack your passport in case we need to get you out of the country?"

"Yes, and everything in me is screaming leave, but I can't, Gwen. Not until those men pay for what they did to Davi." Tiffany's jaw had now set, and her eyes were steely. Gwen admired her cousin's bravery. The resolve on her face brought colour to her cheeks. She patted her arm.

"It's a last resort, but at least we have it if needed," she said. Gwen had been wondering about taking

Tiffany back to the *Coral Queen* as her guest, but as she had no idea how powerful this police detective was, she couldn't risk it right now. The cruise line would be obliged to give her cousin up if he made her an international fugitive and murder suspect. Gwen's mind ran through the different ways each scenario could play out, and none of them were positive.

6

This would not be the telephone conversation with Graham that Gwen had hoped for. All the holiday vibes had disappeared as her fingers hovered over the number in her contact list. She pressed the call button, and he answered immediately.

"Hello, Gwen. Did you forget something?" Graham's voice brimmed with optimism, suggesting he was pleased to hear from her.

Gwen inhaled, then exhaled, striving to sound calm and in control, but she couldn't hide the urgency in her voice. "Graham, something terrible has happened. I can't explain over the phone."

"Is your cousin all right?"

"Sort of. Please, I know it's asking a lot, but can you meet us? We're at the Hilton Hotel."

"Of course, but—"

"I'll meet you in the lobby and explain everything when you get here."

"Okay, give me a bit of time to bring Janet up to speed with what's going on here, and I'll be there within the hour. Will that be soon enough?"

"Yes. Thanks, Graham, I'll see you soon."

Gwen ended the call, nodding at Tiffany, who paced the floor nearby. The hotel lobby was a mélange of colours and exotic scents, with striking red and gold accents adorning the walls and plush cushions scattered across the seats. Large potted palms flanked the entrance, their verdant leaves swaying gently in the air-conditioned breeze, but Gwen was more interested in who was entering. With no signs of danger or the man they had seen entering the police station, she allowed herself to breathe.

Christmas decorations were everywhere, more so than at the Taj Samudra. A huge floor-to-ceiling Christmas tree dominated the lobby. The sight of it made her homesick for the *Coral Queen*, where a tree would soon adorn the ship's main atrium. Despite the beauty surrounding them and the sense of the season, Gwen couldn't shake the chill in her spine. She continued scanning the room, looking for any sign of the man Tiffany had told her was a killer.

Gwen ushered Tiffany to a comfortable sofa, which provided a good view of the entrance.

"Are you sure the lobby is the best place to wait?" Tiffany clutched her shoulder bag tightly to her chest. Her green eyes darted around nervously. Gwen felt the same fear, but there was nothing else they could do.

"Trust me," Gwen said, exhaling slowly. "It's better to be in a public place where we can monitor our surroundings and hide in plain sight."

Tiffany nodded, forcing out a shaky breath. "Thanks, Gwen. I don't know what I'd do without you right now."

Gwen placed a comforting hand on her cousin's arm. "We're family, Tiff. We'll get through this. My friend should be here soon, I promise. Graham has a lot of contacts. He'll find a way to keep you safe." She hoped her voice sounded more convincing than she felt.

They waited in the lobby for what seemed to Gwen like an eternity. Every cackle or loud voice caused Gwen's head to turn, her senses on high alert as she watched for Graham. A bang from a falling suitcase made the two of them jump.

Other than when something made her start, Tiffany was quiet, biting her nails every so often.

Although Gwen felt they must have looked like deer in headlights, nobody took any notice of them. The hotel was filled with tourists coming and going. Thankfully, she hadn't seen any cruise ship passengers she recognised. And unless they had cause to enter the medical centre, they wouldn't notice her, especially out of uniform. Gwen's stomach gurgled. She hadn't eaten since breakfast, not even nibbling on the biscuits that came with her coffee at the Taj Samudra. She had resisted, thinking she and Tiffany would enjoy a pleasant lunch. Now, it was well past lunchtime.

Relief washed over Gwen when she caught sight of Graham. True to his word, he entered the hotel lobby forty-five minutes after her call. Like an oasis in a desert, his tall frame and fair hair instantly brought solace. He looked around anxiously and strode towards them when she waved.

"Sorry to keep you waiting," he said, out of breath. "I came as quickly as I could."

"Thanks for coming at all," Gwen said. "This is my cousin, Tiffany. Tiff, this is my friend and colleague, Dr Graham Bentley."

"Call me Graham." He held out his hand, and Tiffany shook it.

"Do you mind if we go through to the restaurant? Neither of us has eaten." Graham took the cue from

Gwen and followed them into a quiet restaurant serving light snacks.

Once seated, a waiter appeared, and Gwen ordered vegetable samosas and bottled water. Tiffany chose a selection of meaty snacks, and Graham opted for a light curry. As soon as the waiter left, his concerned eyes settled on Gwen's. "What's going on?"

Gwen wasted no time explaining the situation, her words sparing no detail. As she spoke, she watched his face shift from confusion to deepening concern. Gwen lowered her voice. "So that about sums it up. There's a man's body in Tiff's condo, and for all we know, the police could have put out a warrant for her arrest."

"From what you say, I doubt it. It sounds as if they want to keep Tiffany in fear and are unlikely to go back for the body in broad daylight."

"That's what I thought too, but I'm worried in case they grow impatient."

They stopped speaking for a few minutes while food was served.

"The way I see it, you're not safe in Colombo," Graham said, looking at Tiffany.

"We need to get you out of the city before these people realise you're gone."

"But where to?" Tiffany asked. "Tempting as it

would be, I can't leave the country until that man and his sidekick pay for Davi's death."

"You might have to leave," said Graham. "But for now, I might be able to arrange for you to stay with someone I know... or used to know... in Kandy." Graham polished off his curry and rose from the table. "Give me a few minutes."

Gwen and Tiffany picked at their food and drank water.

"I'm amazed I can eat at all," said Tiffany.

"You'll need to keep your strength up," said Gwen, pleased that her cousin had managed to eat something. She herself was struggling, but her stomach told her she must eat.

Graham strode back to the table and took his seat, a dullness in his eyes. Gwen's heart sank.

He threw back the rest of his water. "I'm sorry to say, my old friend passed away recently, but all is not lost. After I explained Tiffany's predicament, without going into too much detail, his widow has agreed for us to go over there. Let's have coffee and then we should leave as soon as possible." Graham requested coffee while Gwen and Tiffany finished eating.

Gwen had been tempted to leave straight away but, in retrospect, appreciated the caffeine. Graham insisted on settling the bill, and Gwen was too tired to argue.

"Wait," said Gwen when they got outside, "Tiffany, we need to get rid of your phone in case they try to track you. Delete everything you can first. How about dropping it back at your condo? It'll be harder for the corrupt detective to trace you without it. We need to hope he'll be cautious about requesting your phone history."

"But what about when they come for the body? They'll grow suspicious."

"Is there anywhere else in the building you can leave it?" Gwen asked.

"There's a gym on the top floor. I can hide it under the treadmill. No-one ever cleans under there. If anyone asks, they'll find out I work out in there and will assume I dropped it."

"That's settled then," Graham said. Tiffany wiped her phone of contacts and messages. "I've forwarded everything important to my cloud," she said, handing it over to Gwen.

"Right, let's do this."

"I should contact my manager, but I daren't."

"When are you due back in?" Gwen asked.

"Not until next week. I took a week's annual leave, knowing you were coming to stay."

"At least no alarm bells will be raised at the hospital," said Graham. "That benefits us. Did you mention Gwen's arrival?"

"No, my manager was off, so I just put the request through, and it was granted."

Gwen heaved an internal sigh of relief. They left the hotel and climbed into Tiffany's car. Gwen shared the back seat with her suitcase. Tiffany was eager to put some distance between themselves and any potential danger, but first they had to stop again at the condo building. Each time they went near the place, they risked being seen. Graham offered to take the phone upstairs, but Tiffany said the fewer people seeing them, the better, so she went inside herself.

Tiffany was shaking when she returned. "I had a brainwave. One of my neighbours is going on holiday to Mumbai today. She'll be away for two weeks. I stopped by her flat to say goodbye and told her I needed to go off-grid for a while. She agreed to take my phone on holiday with her."

"Why would she do that?" Gwen asked, suspicious.

"She's a retired private investigator. Totally trustworthy and doesn't ask questions."

"Brilliant," said Graham. "That buys us some time."

"I checked my apartment. You were right about Davi. His body is still there. Shouldn't I call for an ambulance or something so that someone finds him?"

"Best not," said Graham. "As much as I hate to say it, you're better off letting the criminals move the body rather than incriminating yourself."

"Won't they do that anyway?" Gwen asked.

"I don't think so. At least not initially. They took a tremendous risk shooting a man in front of a foreign national. They won't want to play that hand unless they have to. It's not in their interests to draw attention to Tiffany's story. My guess is any searching they do will be low-key."

The alternative, Gwen knew, was if the killers couldn't get Tiffany to comply, they might dispose of her in the same way as they had Davi.

7

As Tiffany took the A1 following the signs to Kandy, Gwen stared out of the window, shifting her attention to the changing landscape. The late afternoon light softened the terrain, casting a golden-amber glow across the lush countryside. The highway cut through rubber plantations and scattered coconut groves, their broad fronds swaying gently in the tropical breeze.

The air gradually became cooler and less humid as they climbed. Wisps of smoke from small roadside fires drifted across the highway, carrying a faint aroma of burning palm leaves and wood into the car through her half-open window. Roadside vendors' stalls flashed by – displays of bright red rambutans, yellow-green king coconuts, and bunches of small bananas broke through the greenery. Gwen mused how the ship's chefs would be taking delivery of local fruits and other delicacies over the next week to prepare meals for the passengers.

While Graham asked Tiffany about her life and work in Colombo, trying to put her at ease, Gwen's attention oscillated between their conversation and the scenery.

"Australians love to travel. I started in Bali and then went to Indonesia, Malaysia, Thailand, and ended up in Sri Lanka. Then I met a fella just as my money was running out."

"You mentioned him, a Kiwi, wasn't he?" said Gwen.

"Yeah, John. Nice guy, but he wanted to keep travelling. I needed some money, so we agreed to separate. The hospital was desperate for nurses, and I got a work visa and fell in love with the place. Colombo can be beautiful." Tiffany shuddered. "Until recently, when the drug gangs started targeting the hospital. I had no idea how far they were willing to go..." She looked at Gwen through the rearview mirror and then said, "I've only been to Kandy once before. You can already see why it's ideal for tea growing."

Gwen forced a weak smile, accepting the change of subject. "It's beautiful."

They could see tea plantations in the distance, carpeting the hillsides in neat, undulating rows of deep emerald green, their symmetry a testament to colonial agricultural planning.

"Those are called kadé," said Tiffany, pointing to small shops and booths as they passed through a village.

At any other time, Gwen would have asked to stop so they could explore.

As if reading her mind, Tiffany added, "Sorry, this trip is being ruined for you, Gwen."

Gwen had no answer.

"We'll help you through this," said Graham.

"Thanks again for coming, Graham," Gwen said, her voice shakier than intended. "You're the first person I thought of, and you're always reliable in an emergency." The words felt inadequate, but she had to let him know how grateful she was.

"This is a different kind of emergency than I'm used to, that's for sure," he said, forcing a grin. "But I'm pleased you called me."

As they approached the outskirts of Kandy, the road wound more dramatically. Clusters of giant bamboo and wild orchids clung to the rocky roadside, their presence a reminder of Sri Lanka's remarkable biodiversity. Gwen pressed her head against the cool glass. As the landscape continued to impress, she felt envious of how nature carried on, oblivious to human drama. Nature had the ability to just be.

They remained silent for the next thirty minutes while Tiffany followed the directions from Gwen's phone. Graham closed his eyes, and Gwen focused again on the scenery, which helped her compartmentalise what they were running from.

Gwen eventually broke the silence. "Once Tiffany is settled in a safe place, we need a plan to keep her protected. Any ideas?"

"First, let's make sure there is a place to stay where no one can find her," Graham suggested, opening his eyes and looking at both women. "Then we can figure out our next move."

Gwen's heart was burdened with fear for her cousin. Tiffany was strong, but even the strongest person needed support. "Okay," she said.

Tiffany pulled over at the side of the road. "Would one of you mind driving for the last bit? I'm bushed."

They swapped seats, with Tiffany sitting in the back. Gwen moved to the passenger seat while Graham drove.

Tiffany didn't speak, staring out of the window as Gwen had been doing. Gwen could imagine the turmoil going on inside her cousin's mind if her own thoughts mirrored the anxiety Tiffany felt.

"Everything is going to be okay, Tiff," Gwen said,

looking over her shoulder. "We won't let anything happen to you."

Tiffany forced a nod, continuing to stare out of the window. Gwen took the hint and gave her cousin some space.

Graham used Gwen's navigation app to guide them through the last few miles, and the car eventually stopped outside a substantial, white-walled bungalow nestled amidst lush green foliage. The early evening sun filtered through the branches of surrounding trees, casting long shadows on the ground. Gwen felt a sense of peace wash over her as they stepped out of the car.

"This is it," Graham announced, looking around with a nod of approval. "This is Mrs Nalini Bandara's home."

The front door opened, and a petite woman with greying hair appeared on the threshold. She wore a vibrant red floral sari and a welcoming smile that seemed to spread from ear to ear.

"Dr Graham Bentley and friends... Welcome to Kandy," Mrs Bandara's arms were outstretched as she beckoned them inside.

"I'm sorry to intrude, and sorry again to hear of your loss. Ramesh was a good friend, although we'd lost touch," said Graham.

Mrs Bandara waved his sympathy away. "Thank

you. He told me all about you, Dr Graham Bentley. You are one of the good ones, he said." Her eyes moved to Gwen and Tiffany. "I'm Nalini. You must be Gwen and Tiffany. Please, come inside."

"Thank you," Gwen said gratefully. "It's kind of you to let us come here."

"Think nothing of it," Nalini replied, closing the door behind them. The roomy entrance and air-conditioned home were a welcome relief after a cramped drive in Tiffany's tiny car. "Now, before you tell me your story, let me prepare some tea and refreshments."

As they settled into the cosy sitting room, with its see-through curtains, mosquito screens, and embroidered cushions, Gwen was hopeful this would be a safe haven for her cousin. The scent of freshly brewed tea filled the air, mingling with the fragrance of incense from a small Buddhist shrine in the corner.

Nalini set down a tray laden with steaming cups of tea and an assortment of sweet desserts.

"I hope you like strong tea. This is a special blend known for its restorative properties," she said, pouring each of them a cup from a large teapot.

"Thank you," said Graham.

"Just what the doctor ordered," said Gwen.

The others chuckled, appreciating her attempt at humour.

"And these," said Nalini, pointing to the plate of desserts, "are a selection of homemade sweet treats we love in Sri Lanka."

As they each helped themselves to a sweet dessert, Nalini put them at ease by telling them what they were eating.

Gwen found herself relaxing in their friendly hostess's company and couldn't believe how tasty the Pani Walalu, or honey ring, she had chosen was.

Once they had enjoyed the delicious morsels and were drinking tea, which Gwen had to admit had a kick to it, Nalini's eyes settled on Tiffany. "Graham tells me you need refuge. Please, tell me what brings you here?"

Tiffany looked as though she might cry, so Gwen took a deep breath and recounted the events that led them to Kandy. As she spoke, she noticed Nalini's expression shifting from sympathy to resolute determination.

"Tiffany, you can stay with me until you sort things out," she declared when Gwen had finished. "Nobody should have to go through what you have experienced, let alone a kind and dedicated professional like you." Her kind eyes and words made Gwen want to hug her.

"Thank you so much, Mrs Bandara. I'm happy to

pay for my stay," Tiffany whispered, her voice trembling.

"Dear child, there is no need for that, and please call me Nalini," the gentle woman said, placing a comforting hand on Tiffany's shoulder. "Your story resonates with me more than you know. My nephew, Ravindu, lost his life to a drugs overdose several years ago. The pain of losing someone in such circumstances is something I wouldn't wish on anyone else. If I can help you, even in the smallest way, stop these people, that's payment enough for me."

Gwen was grateful to the kind woman offering understanding and empathy, as well as shelter. Graham couldn't have chosen a better place for Tiffany to come to.

Graham excused himself and stepped outside. There, Gwen watched him pace the length of the veranda, knowing that behind those intelligent eyes, a plan was forming. She sipped her tea, feeling the warmth spread through her body as she considered their options.

"Right," said Graham, coming back inside and breaking the comfortable silence. "The first thing we need to do is get closer to the source of this mess. Your friend Davi was a hospital pharmacist, you say?"

Tiffany nodded.

"I mentioned to Gwen this morning that I have another old friend, Ranil Fernando, who works at the National Hospital. He mentioned in one of his more recent emails that the hospital had been experiencing a surge in drug-related deaths, so I think it's safe to assume he's not involved."

"That sounds like a good place to start. Perhaps he has an inkling about who's supplying drugs," said Gwen.

"He didn't mention drugs being stolen, which is odd, but there's only so much you can put in an email," Graham said. "As I mentioned, I dropped him an email saying we would be held up in Colombo for repairs, and he replied, offering me a tour of the hospital and suggesting we meet for dinner. I propose that Gwen and I pay him a visit as interested health professionals, which, in part, we are because I planned to do so anyway." He looked at Gwen. "Under happier circumstances, but it is what it is. We can access the hospital through Ranil without raising any suspicions."

"Then it's settled," Gwen said, feeling much more positive with the bones of a plan in place. "We'll visit the hospital and see what we can uncover. We also have the patient we admitted to the hospital this morning."

"Of course! Even better," said Graham. "We can

visit Mr Thompson as well, and no-one will be any the wiser."

Gwen turned to Tiffany, whose face was pale. "We'll do everything we can to help you, Tiff. I promise."

"Thanks," she said, "although I have mixed feelings about it. Please be careful." Tears glistened in her eyes.

"We will," Gwen grinned. "What can go wrong?" she added, trying to lighten the mood. But as she wrapped Tiffany in a warm embrace, she felt less than confident about playing amateur detective.

"Might I suggest you all stay here tonight? I always have far more food than I can eat, and it's getting late," said Nalini. "The street lighting between here and Colombo is not always the best."

"I didn't bring a change of clothes," said Graham.

"You're about Ramesh's size. You can wear something of his. He would have wanted me to help you," she said.

"In that case, I'll pop outside and call my deputy to let her know she's in charge for the night. I will have to get back to the ship first thing, so we'll need to leave early, if that's okay with you, Gwen?"

"The earlier, the better." Gwen was keen to do what had to be done. She might be frightened, but she was determined to help her cousin.

8

"Take care of yourself, Tiff," Gwen whispered into her cousin's ear. "We'll stay in touch."

Tiffany clung to Gwen, her voice tremulous. "Thanks, Gwen. Be careful, okay? I couldn't bear it if something happened to you."

"Nobody knows about my link to you, and we have a credible plan that won't arouse suspicion, but we'll be extra cautious. I promise." Gwen pulled away from the embrace and looked into Tiffany's eyes. "Remember, you're an Aussie. You'll come out of this a stronger person." With a nod from Tiffany, Gwen moved away and joined Graham.

Nalini's dark brown eyes were warm and knowing. The older lady rested a hand on Gwen's shoulder. "Trust your instincts," she whispered. "Both of you.

You are skilled and compassionate people, and I know you will find the truth."

"I hope so," said Gwen.

"Wait a moment." Nalini went back inside the house, returning with a set of car keys, which she handed to Graham. "Leave Tiffany's car in my garage and take Ramesh's car. I don't drive these days." Tears threatened to spill from Nalini's eyes.

"But—"

"You don't want these people to recognise that car." Nalini motioned towards the Mini.

Nalini was right. Graham swallowed his objection, taking the keys from their host's hands.

Gwen hugged Nalini. "We appreciate your help more than words can express."

"Do not worry about Tiffany. She will be safe with me. All anyone will know is that she is the daughter of one of Ramesh's old friends come to stay for a holiday. We often had foreign visitors when my husband was alive."

Graham looked at Nalini. "When we return, I hope it will be under better circumstances," he told her. "We'll call you."

"I look forward to both." Nalini Bandara shooed them away. "Now go."

Gwen turned to Graham, shrugging her shoulders. They would need to rely on each other now more than ever. Graham thanked Nalini. While he drove an old black BMW out of the garage, Gwen moved the Mini inside. She locked the car and the garage, returning the keys to Nalini before climbing into the passenger seat. Gwen cast one last glance back at the house where her cousin would remain in hiding until they had achieved the daunting task ahead of them. Nalini and Tiffany waved from the front garden.

"Everything is going to be all right," she whispered, more to herself than to Graham.

His hands gripped the steering wheel. "We'll do our best to bring these people down," he said. "And if we can't, we'll find a way to get Tiffany out of Sri Lanka and convince her it's the right thing to do."

Gwen murmured in the affirmative, thinking about whether they could offer Tiffany a temporary job on board the *Coral Queen*.

With a slow exhale, Graham pulled into traffic, heading for the outskirts of Kandy and the road to Colombo. As they drove away, the sun rose behind the horizon, casting early-morning shadows across the road.

"Do you really think we can get to the bottom of this?" Gwen asked, her eyes focused on the road ahead.

"We can try."

"For Davi, for Tiffany, for Nalini's nephew, and for everyone who's been hurt by these people, we'll do it."

"You realise we might not be able to, though, Gwen," said Graham. "We don't know how much deeper the corruption goes."

"I can't think like that at the moment. Tiffany's terrified, but she's also stubborn. She won't leave unless her friend's killers are brought to justice, and if they're not, I'm petrified she'll end up dead."

Graham patted her arm. "That will not happen. We'll do everything we can, Gwen."

Most of the journey passed in comfortable silence, and the car hummed along as if it were brand new. It might have been old, but it hadn't been used much and was in pristine condition, not to mention having a full tank of petrol. Graham stopped in front of the port entrance. "She drives like a dream," he said, climbing out but leaving the engine running.

Gwen walked around to the driver's side and got in. "I'll find a car park to put it out of sight and then check in at a hostel somewhere. You take care of your duties," she said.

"Are you sure that's what you want to do?" She knew he wasn't happy about her intention to stay in Colombo.

"As far as the team is concerned, I'm on holiday. It will be best not to let on that anything's changed."

Graham sighed, "Okay, I'll call you. We'll meet at midday. Janet's taking the morning to do some sightseeing."

"I'll text you when I've found somewhere."

Twenty minutes later, Gwen had parked the car in a long-stay underground car park and after checking the map on her phone, she entered the dimly lit YMCA International Guesthouse. Exhaustion tugged at every muscle of her body. Despite the comfort of one of Nalini's spare beds the night before, she had not slept. They had driven for three and a half hours straight after leaving at 5 am.

"Do you have a room for one?" Gwen asked the woman at the desk.

"How long will you be staying?"

"Six nights," Gwen replied, giving a random answer because she had no idea how long it would take, and that was the extent of her leave. She observed the eclectic mix of guests filing in and out and the feeble attempt at Christmas décor around the place.

The woman quoted a price that seemed reasonable for what Gwen assumed would be basic accommodation. Tiffany had mentioned that the YMCA International was a haven and central to the city. Both of which were required. She was pleased they had space for her.

"Here are your keys," the receptionist said, handing her a key ring with two keys.

"One opens the front door. Don't lose it or we charge for a new one. Take the third door on the left." The woman inclined her head towards a corridor.

"Thank you," said Gwen. She turned in the direction she had been pointed to, pulling the suitcase behind her. *I'm going to have to buy a small travel bag and store the suitcase somewhere or dispense with some of my belongings,* she thought. When she opened the door to the room, she was weary but satisfied that she had passed herself off as one of the many Australian tourists who travel through Asia. Once inside, Gwen locked the door and switched on the overhead fan. The room was as she had imagined, basic, with a double bed, but cleaner than expected. It made a perfect place to hide for a while.

Her phone rang. She tapped the answer. "Hello Graham, I've checked in at the YMCA International; all good so far."

There was silence on the other end, and for a moment, Gwen thought they had been cut off. "You won't like it, but I caught Janet before she went out, and told her what's going on," he said. "I know you didn't want me to, but I need the flexibility to come and go without drawing attention to the fact. Janet's sensible and can keep a secret."

Gwen had suspected it would be difficult for Graham to mislead his friend and colleague. He had other responsibilities, and it was only right he maintain trust with his deputy. "It's the right thing to do," she said.

His exhale made his relief palpable. "Thanks. On another note, you know we talked about the team staffing situation?"

"Huh?"

"I've spoken to Peter and suggested we take advantage of our extended stay. He's agreed we can take on a locum through the cruise line's agency. Truth is, we're getting to the stage where we need extra staff anyway. I caught him at the right moment. The team had a lot to deal with last night, so he was fine with someone coming aboard for a trial run. The agency had just the right person waiting in the wings. Janet and I will be responsible for him, and he comes highly recommended: a chap called Chamara Munasinghe."

"Wow!" Gwen was taken aback at both the speed of the decision, and the availability of a medic. She was used to being involved in major decisions and would have argued for an extra nurse or a nurse and a nursing assistant, but now was not the time to be churlish. "You don't hang around, do you? I look forward to meeting him."

"I'm sorry, Gwen, but I'd feel incredibly guilty bailing on the team, and it means I can take more shore leave without it looking suspicious and without putting Janet under too much stress. Even though we've got a reduced passenger list with the cruise line offering to put passengers up in hotels for Christmas, there's still a lot to do."

"Yeah, I get it. It's a good idea," she said. *So why do I feel disappointed?*

Graham pressed on. "I'm going to let the rest of the team know about the recruit at lunchtime. Janet's given up the rest of her shore leave to free me up. It means I'll be later getting off the ship today than expected. I should be with you around two, after seeing the new guy in an hour. I'll show him round and introduce him to the captain. Janet will be back by lunchtime, and we can introduce him to the team together."

"I don't suppose he's worked at the Colombo National?" Gwen's mind returned to the job at hand.

"Not that I know of. I'll ask him. He'd already been vetted and interviewed via head office and has worked in various casualty departments in remote parts of the community, as far as I've been told. He'll be a good fit."

"Great."

Graham took the hint and changed the subject. "What's the guesthouse like?"

"Basic, but clean, and close to the city centre. Seeing as you're going to be delayed, I'll head over to the National and check the lie of the land with a visit to Mr Thompson."

"Good idea. We'll meet later, and then I'll contact Ranil."

"Okay. I'll see you in the main reception between two and three. Text me if you're going to be late."

"I will. Be careful, Gwen."

"No worries," she said. "See you this afternoon." Gwen let out a long sigh after the call ended. She was torn between her responsibilities on board the *Coral Queen*, irritation at being left out of a major decision, and her responsibility to her cousin. It wasn't a situation she would have chosen to be in, but she was here, and she had made a promise. The image of Tiffany's executed friend lying on her condo floor haunted her waking thoughts. That's where her priorities must lie.

9

On her way to the hospital, Gwen navigated thronging crowds while passing numerous street vendors, each calling for attention. Christmas preparations were in full swing, which still surprised her, given that Sri Lanka was mainly Buddhist. If she hadn't been so burdened by the unwelcome mantle she carried, it would have been a pleasure to revel in the atmosphere. She pictured herself with Tiffany entering shops and stopping to browse at street vendor offerings. Thinking of Tiffany pushed her onwards. Increasing her pace, Gwen ignored the call to shop.

The National Hospital of Sri Lanka was a sprawling complex of white concrete buildings set amid lush greenery. Gwen had used a map app on her phone to locate the hospital, which occupied a prime spot in central Colombo along E. W. Perera Mawatha. Small gardens and courtyards divided the grounds, where flowering frangipani trees perfumed the air and red-vented bulbuls nested in the foliage. She recognised the birds from cruise stops in India and knew they were common in Sri Lanka as well. Medical students in white coats gathered under the shelter of massive banyan trees, no doubt on a break from lectures. The hospital's accident and emergency department was housed in a newer wing with gleaming glass panels and buzzed with constant activity as ambulances navigated the circular driveway under the covered entrance.

The temperature, though mild for this part of the world, was hot, and Gwen used a handkerchief to wipe away the sweat forming on her forehead. The sun cast bright highlights on the hospital's façade. Hosts of people milled about outside the main entrance; a few were crying, others paced, and some held hands with loved ones while waiting. Cigarette smoke formed a cloud close to the entrance where smokers congregated.

As Gwen stepped inside, she paused to get her bearings, looking and listening. Familiar hospital sounds greeted her. Voices echoed off the walls. Through the bustle, the sound of heeled shoes making their way through the corridors clacked against the floors, though hidden beneath saris. Porters pushed trolleys and wheelchairs, and there were occasional announcements over the PA system. Gwen took a deep breath before navigating her way through the crowd to her destination. Medical staff in worn white coats traversed the main corridor as people stepped aside to let them pass. Nurses wearing smart white starched aprons fastened in a cross at the back called out the names of patients.

Gwen approached the reception desk and waited in a disordered queue to speak to the woman behind it. Eventually, she squeezed through a gap and got the receptionist's attention.

"Excuse me, can you tell me which ward Mr Benjamin Thompson was admitted to?"

"Just one moment, please." Gwen was relieved when the woman replied in English. After tapping a few keys, her eyes scrunched to concentrate on her computer screen, she turned back to Gwen. "Are you a relative?"

"No, I'm the senior nurse from the cruise ship Mr Thompson was travelling on before being admitted," Gwen said, smiling.

"I see." The woman returned her attention to the computer before raising her head. "Found him! He's on Ward 17. That's on the third floor. You'll find signage in English to follow."

"Thank you," said Gwen before starting her journey along the labyrinthine corridors. The receptionist was right about the signs. They were in English and two other languages. One, she assumed, was Sinhalese and the other Tamil. Taking a lift to the third floor, Gwen mulled over what had happened in just two days, and the reality set in. Horrified and nervous about being caught up in a web of murder and conspiracy, everything within her screamed, run!

The lift stopped at each floor, where more people crammed in, making it hard to breathe. It was well over capacity by the time the doors opened on the third floor.

Glad to be out of the packed lift, she followed a family to the surgical ward. Gwen hung back, hesitating for a moment before pushing the doors open. The ward was comfortingly familiar, with the steady rhythms of beeping machines and the quiet murmur of conversation between patients and staff. The air was heavy with the smell of antiseptic. Gwen approached the nurse behind a desk.

Gwen hoped the staff spoke as good English as the receptionist. "Hello, my name is Gwen Sumner. I'm a senior nurse from the *Coral Queen* cruise ship. I understand you have a passenger of ours, Mr Benjamin Thompson?"

The nurse, who appeared to be in her early thirties, had a friendly smile and buck teeth that suited her face. "Yes, we have Mr Thompson. Would you like to see him?"

"Yes, please," said Gwen. "Were we right in assuming it was appendicitis?"

The nurse gave her a wide grin. "He had his appendix removed yesterday afternoon. I was going to contact your team today, as his daughter would like to get him back to the ship before you set sail again."

"That would be wonderful," said Gwen. "The ship's undergoing repairs, so I'm sure we can make that possible."

"Good. I'll make a note of it. If you're happy, he should be ready for discharge in a few days. Thank you for saving me the trouble of contacting you. I'm Rutvi. Follow me, and I'll show you where he is."

"What a beautiful name," said Gwen.

"Thank you."

Rutvi led Gwen to a bed, beside which Mr Thompson was sitting in a chair reading a book.

"Mr Thompson?" Gwen whispered. He looked up, and his face lit up.

"Sister Sumner! What brings you here?"

"I'll leave you to it," said Rutvi.

"Thank you." Gwen pulled up a chair to sit next to him. Although the visit was a ruse, she was delighted to see him looking so well. "I wanted to check on you. The nurse told me you had your appendix removed."

"Yes. You and Dr Bentley were spot on. Appendicitis. Young Rutvi there was going to contact you to ask if you'd be happy to take me back in a couple of days."

"I've told her we'll be glad to once they're happy to let you go, and you feel well enough."

Mr Thompson's blue eyes brightened, and his entire face crinkled into a grin. "Apart from a very sore side, I'm doing fine, Sister. The staff have been amazing. In fact, the surgeon's not long left after his ward round. They all speak perfect English, you know?"

Gwen thought Mr Thompson looked and sounded remarkably well following surgery at the ripe old age of eighty-three. She scanned the ward. Calm efficiency was how she would describe it. As their conversation continued, Gwen noticed a man lying in the next bed. His arms bore visible tramlines, hinting at a history of drug use. He was struggling to reach a glass of water on the bedside table.

"Excuse me a minute, Mr Thompson," Gwen said, turning her attention to the man. "Let me help you with that," she said, taking the glass and topping it up with water from a jug. She handed it to him.

The man sagged back against his pillows, relief etched into his sunken features. He spoke in broken English. "Thank you. No strength in my hands. My fault." His gaze dropped to his lap, shame giving an edge to his voice.

"I'm Gwen, and this is Benjamin," said Gwen.

"I know Ben. He had a knife." The man's voice was raspy, and he sounded exhausted as he mock-sliced his lower right side with a finger. "Sim Kumar."

"You were asleep when they came round with hot drinks, Sim. Do you want me to ask them to get you one?" Mr Thompson asked.

"No, thank you. Water will be fine," Sim replied.

"Can I do anything else for you, Sim?" Gwen asked.

The frail man took a gulp of water. "You've done plenty, ma'am. Few people show me kindness. But I don't deserve it."

"What makes you say that?"

"I've brought pain and shame on myself. I used to work here – porter. But bad people came." Sim held out his arms to show the tramlines.

Gwen nodded. "I'm sorry to hear that," she said.

"Don't be sorry, ma'am. I lost my job, but I'm determined not to go back to that life, not now the doctors saved me. They took a kidney but gave me my life."

"Will you get support when you leave here?"

"Yes. My sister has promised to help me when I'm ready." He smiled. "She says she'll help me put on weight."

Gwen was happy to hear it. Sim was emaciated and in need of tender loving care.

"I'm glad you have someone to support your recuperation," she said.

"Not that I deserve her help. I have many regrets – I wish I'd seen through those people."

"What people?" asked Gwen.

Sim looked around as if worried that someone was listening. Satisfied that they weren't, he said, "Drug crime happens here, right under the authorities' noses."

"Have you told anyone about this?"

"I did, but it goes high." Sim pointed to the ceiling for emphasis. "The minute I exposed what was happening, I was out."

"They fired you?"

Sim nodded.

"When you say this crime goes high up, how high?" Gwen asked, feeling a chill when Sim's eyes widened in alarm. He was looking over her shoulder, and his hands trembled as he turned away from her, rolling onto his side.

Gwen turned around to see what was disturbing the frail man. Her breath caught in her throat. There, at the nurses' station, stood the detective Tiffany had pointed out – the one who had shot her friend Davi. He was speaking in low tones to Rutvi, his presence creating tension among the other nurses, who backed away from him. A porter's hands shook as he passed the detective, the glasses on the tray he carried clinking together as he hurriedly avoided the man at the desk.

Sim muttered under his breath. "You'd better go back to Ben."

Gwen reluctantly sat back down. She could barely take her eyes off the detective, whose posture was rigid and jaw set tight. He radiated simmering aggression that made her skin prickle. She sensed he was a storm ready to break.

"Who is that man?" Mr Thompson whispered.

"I'm not sure," said Gwen, her voice sounding steadier than she felt.

Sim turned onto his back, murmuring, "de Silva. Detective Rohan de Silva. Don't be friendly to me in front of him. And don't trust him." Sim's voice had lost the hope injected by their earlier conversation.

When she saw de Silva approaching, Gwen's heart

hammered against her chest. How could he have found her? Mr Thompson engaged in small talk, and Gwen tried to follow suit, feeling breathless.

de Silva had flint-like brown eyes, was clean-shaven with light brown skin and cropped black hair. His suit screamed designer. Gwen guessed he was around her age, about forty-five. She forced a smile, but de Silva glanced menacingly at them. Relief flooded through her when she realised he wasn't here for her. He drew the curtains around Sim's bed aggressively. There was no mistaking the fear in Sim's eyes before the curtain hid him from view. de Silva was both arrogant and crooked. Gwen felt guilty for her relief.

"Excuse me, sir, I need to talk to you," de Silva was speaking for their benefit; she was certain of that.

Gwen looked down the ward, hoping a nurse would intervene, but none did.

The one-sided conversation behind the curtain was in Sinhalese, so Gwen couldn't make out what was being said. However, the tone was all too clear, threatening and merciless.

Once de Silva left, Sim clammed up, pretending to be asleep, but his shaking sheets betrayed the fact that he was very much awake. Gwen glared angrily after the detective, who stopped to have another conversation with Rutvi. She looked away when de Silva pointed towards her and Mr Thompson.

Mr Thompson lowered his voice. “That detective’s a nasty piece of work. I’ll ask Sim what it was all about later. I bet he’s one of these high-up crooks.”

Gwen didn’t tell him what was going on but nodded. “You may be right, Mr Thompson. And that might be useful.” She needed to know what de Silva had said to Sim and whether he could help them expose the gang responsible for Davi’s death.

“Call me Ben if we’re going to be working together.” He gave her a wink.

She couldn’t help smiling. “I’m meeting with Dr Bentley shortly. I’m sure he’d like to come and see how you’re getting on,” she said.

“Come anytime, Sister,” Mr Thompson replied. “You know where I’ll be.”

“Good to see you looking so well, Ben,” she said.

“Don’t worry, Sister. I’ve got this.” He inclined his head towards Sim.

Before leaving the ward, Gwen stopped by the nurse’s station and thanked Rutvi. “Our patient is singing your praises,” she said.

“That’s good to hear.”

“The patient in the bed next to him seemed a little shaken after his visitor,” said Gwen. “Who was that man?”

Rutvi frowned. “I’m not at liberty to say much about his visit, but he’s a detective. He asked who you were and what you were doing here.”

Gwen was startled.

“Don’t be concerned. He’s suspicious by nature. I explained you were visiting a passenger from your ship. Just be thankful you’re not in any trouble.”

Gwen forced a laugh. “Good to know. I might visit again later. I’m meeting our chief medical officer. He has an old friend who works here. Here’s my mobile number in case you need to contact me about Mr Thompson’s discharge. It’ll save you hanging around while they try to find someone for you to speak to.”

“Thanks,” said Rutvi, taking the card and stapling it to a file. She scribbled a number onto a piece of paper. “This is a direct line to the ward.”

“Thank you, Rutvi. Hopefully, I’ll see you again,” said Gwen, taking the piece of paper and placing it in her handbag.

It took tremendous effort to stroll from the ward as if she didn’t have a care, while feeling like a mountain of dread had settled on her shoulders.

10

The sight of Graham strolling through the doors into the main reception filled Gwen with relief. Her heart gave a surprising flutter.

Graham's wide smile when he saw her and the sparkle in his eyes took her by surprise. "Hello, Gwen. I hope I haven't kept you waiting."

"Not long; I just got here."

"Have you had time to eat?"

Gwen shook her head. "I knew you wouldn't get the chance, so I waited. There's a public café with the most enticing aromas along that corridor." She motioned to her right.

"In that case, may I take you to lunch?" Graham held out his arm, and she looped hers through it.

"Why not?"

The café served a mix of Sri Lankan and European cuisine. They chose dishes from the former, having both acquired a taste for Asian food. It appeared it was mostly visitors who used the café; perhaps the staff had their own canteen. Gwen looked across the table at Graham as he ate. If circumstances were different, she could get used to being with this man, she mused before giving herself an immediate internal slap. *No way, Sumner. You're not going down that road.*

"Did you see Mr Thompson?" Graham asked.

"I did. He's had his appendix removed and looks really well. The nurse said they could discharge him back to the ship in a few days. I gave her my mobile number."

"Excellent. I expect his daughter will be pleased."

"Apparently so. I also had the fright of my life."

"Did someone collapse?"

"No. There's a man in the bed next to Ben – Mr Thompson told me to call him that – who is terrified of the detective who shot Tiffany's friend."

"How do you know?"

"The detective, Rohan de Silva, showed up. I don't mind admitting that by the look on his face when he headed our way, I thought he'd discovered who I was and what I was doing."

"There's no way he could have done that in such a short time."

"I know, but it was a scary moment all the same. Anyway, the man next door to Ben, named Sim, is an ex-porter and sadly a former junkie. He was about to tell us about the drugs issue at the hospital, which goes high up, when de Silva paid him a visit."

Graham raised an eyebrow, frowning. "Did the detective say anything to you?"

"No, he just glared. He's an aggressive-looking beast, dressed well above his pay grade. Rutvi, the ward nurse, told me he asked about us, and when she mentioned I was visiting Ben, a patient from a docked cruise ship, he showed no further interest."

"Phew! That could have been dangerous."

Gwen had certainly felt tense at the time, but there was no reason for de Silva to connect her to Tiffany. "Ben's figured out something is going on and is determined to help. He's going to speak to Sim. I didn't tell him anything because I don't want to put him in danger. It'll come across as idle curiosity that way."

Graham concentrated on his food for the next five minutes. His eyes looked tired.

"I'm sorry for dragging you into this mess," she said.

"It would be worse if you hadn't. I've been

thinking of ways to get your cousin out of Sri Lanka. If I speak to Peter, I'm sure we could offer her a short-term job and drop her off in Australia."

Gwen shook her head. "The thought crossed my mind as well, but you saw how she reacted. Tiffany baulked at any suggestion of leaving before justice is served for her friend."

"And I told her she may have to leave. It won't be easy to get this man, de Silva, arrested, Gwen. We still don't know where this journey will lead us."

"Further than we thought, according to Sim. He tried to blow the whistle and got sacked from the hospital, which suggests someone in authority here is involved. I expect de Silva's visit today was to warn him to keep his mouth shut."

"When you can't call on the police, it becomes very dangerous. What happens if this de Silva comes after us?"

"We go back to the *Coral Queen* and ask Waverley to put a call through to Interpol or something."

Graham grinned. "You're becoming a natural."

Gwen felt the exact opposite, but she couldn't leave her cousin with her life in danger. "Maybe Nalini can talk some sense into my cousin."

"We'll phone tonight and ask her to try," said Graham. "In the meantime, I suggest we pay my old friend a visit and see what he can tell us. Let's try to keep it natural. I don't want to spook him."

Gwen finished her last mouthful of sweet and spicy mango curry and washed it down with the remains of a bottle of sparkling spring water. "I hope your friend can help." She didn't dare suggest that Graham's friend might be part of a conspiracy.

As if reading her mind, Graham said, "Ranil might well know something about the Sri Lankan drug trade. As I said, he mentioned he was concerned in a recent email, but he's not involved, Gwen." Graham wiped his mouth with a napkin. "We were close during our medical training in London. I haven't met him in years, but he's a good sort. We've always kept in touch via email."

"He could be the perfect person to help," Gwen said, her heart filled with a mixture of hope and concern. "But we need to be careful not to arouse suspicion."

"Agreed," Graham replied, his brows furrowing. "Time to play the interested visitors. Are you ready?"

"Yep. I guess so."

"We'll speak to someone at the front desk and ask them to page him. Let's hope he's available. If not, we'll come back tomorrow."

"Your friendship is a plus. We'll see if it's strong

enough for him to confide in you if we get that far," Gwen said.

"Ranil's one of the good guys. He always had a good heart, even when we were getting up to mischief," Graham said, his eyes tinged with nostalgia.

Gwen and Graham headed to the hospital's main reception, where a different woman from the one Gwen had spoken to earlier was on duty.

Graham spoke to her briefly, explaining who they were and asking her to page his old friend. He seemed tense.

The receptionist answered the telephone when it rang. "Hello Dr Fernando, I have a Dr Graham Bentley at reception. He's asking if it's possible to see you?"

The receptionist handed Graham the phone.

"Graham? Is that really you?"

"Hello, Ranil. It's been a long time."

Gwen waited patiently while the two men exchanged pleasantries. Graham was clearly waiting for the opportunity to get to the point.

"Actually, Ranil, I'm here with our chief nurse, Gwen Sumner. I know it's a cheek, but you said if I had time while in Sri Lanka, I should look you up. Could we meet at a convenient time to tour your hospital?"

"Now? Yes, that would be perfect. Shall we come to you? Okay. We'll wait here."

Graham handed the telephone back to the receptionist before turning to Gwen, his face beaming. "He's on his way down."

"Wonderful," said Gwen, feeling suddenly nervous.

They hovered by reception, careful not to interrupt the receptionist as she attended to her duties. The phone rang incessantly, and her time alternated between speaking to visitors at the desk and answering calls. No wonder Rutvi gave me the ward's direct line, Gwen thought.

"Graham Bentley!" The voice reached Gwen's ears above the commotion around them. Gwen and Graham turned towards the voice to see a grinning doctor with wavy grey hair, wearing a white coat over a checked shirt and navy-blue tie, heading their way. His eyes crinkled at the corners, evidence of years spent laughing and smiling. As far as Gwen could tell, it wasn't the face of a criminal.

The two men embraced until Graham pulled away, gesturing to Gwen. "This is my friend and colleague, Gwen Sumner."

"Ah, the mysterious friend you mentioned in your emails," Ranil said, winking at Graham.

Gwen noticed a slight reddening of Graham's face

as Ranil took her hand, shaking it warmly. "It's a pleasure to meet you, Gwen."

"Likewise," Gwen replied with a polite smile. It would be hard not to like this man, whom she hoped wasn't involved in any conspiracy.

"Come, let's walk and talk. I'll show you around while we catch up." Ranil gestured for them to follow as he weaved his way through the busy hospital.

As they walked, Ranil regaled Gwen with stories of his and Graham's shared past in London. *Was it the excitement of seeing Graham that made him behave like an ostrich on steroids, or was he always like this?* Ranil recounted late-night study sessions and the misadventures of youth.

"Remember that time we snuck into that exclusive party at the medical society?" Ranil laughed, his eyes twinkling with mischief. "We ended up sharing a drink with one of the keynote speakers – and he never knew we were just students!"

Graham chuckled. "Those were the days. Less pressure, that's for sure. How are things with you? It can't be easy being a hospital consultant."

Ranil's expression grew more serious. "It has its challenges, but doesn't every job? Even yours."

Graham grinned. "As you say, even mine is challenging sometimes."

Gwen and Graham followed Ranil along another

busy corridor, doing their best to keep up with his brisk pace. The scent of antiseptic was strong as they passed the operating theatres. There was also a distant hum of medical machinery and the clattering of porters transporting patients from A to B. Gwen's eyes moved around, recognising the flurry of activity as nurses and doctors hurried past them, each on their own mission to save lives... or eat lunch, she mused.

"How many patients do you treat here daily?" Gwen asked.

"It varies," Ranil replied, barely looking back as he continued to lead them forward.

"But I would say my team averages around two hundred patients a day."

Gwen noticed Graham nodding thoughtfully. She could tell he was contemplating how to steer the conversation to their intended topic.

"That's a lot," he remarked sympathetically.

"My team does most of the work," Ranil said, a note of pride entering his voice.

"Anyone I know?" Graham asked.

"Not in my team, but there is someone you might remember, Graham," Ranil said. "Imran Malik – he was in our year at medical school. He's a brilliant vascular surgeon now, one of the best."

"Imran! Of course I remember him," Graham exclaimed. "It's been years since our paths crossed."

As they rounded a corner, Gwen noticed a shorter man in his early fifties, wearing a cream suit she recognised as Armani, and hand-crafted Italian loafers. He was engaged in an intense, whispered conversation with a nurse who seemed in awe of him. Something about his behaviour and the way he leaned into the nurse's personal space made Gwen's skin crawl with professional disapproval.

"What a coincidence. There he is."

When Ranil called out, Gwen observed the other man's shoulders tense before he turned. His carefully dyed brown hair – a clear attempt to mask grey – shone under the bright corridor lighting as he shifted.

"Imran, look who I've got with me?" The surgeon had darker skin than Ranil, and Gwen noted a flash of annoyance cross his face before he forced a smile. The nurse scurried away, unnoticed by Imran.

"I'm sorry. Have we met before?" His tone was clipped, almost dismissive.

"It's been a long time," Graham said, extending his hand in greeting. "Graham Bentley. We were in the same year." The handshake was perfunctory. Gwen sensed that Imran Malik was not as pleased to see Graham as Ranil was.

"Oh yes. I remember now. Good to see you again." Imran's smile was strained. "And who is this?" As he focused on her, Gwen felt herself being assessed. His forced smile didn't soften his dark eyes.

"This is my friend and colleague, Gwen Sumner. We both work on the *Coral Queen*."

Imran scratched his head.

"It's a cruise ship," said Ranil.

"Oh, I see. I've seen a few in port on my way in to work this week. Are you a doctor, Gwen?"

"No. I'm the senior nurse."

Imran couldn't suppress a condescending curl of his lips. She forced herself to ignore it. "It's a pleasure to meet you, Mr Malik. Or is it customary to call surgeons 'doctor' in Sri Lanka?"

"It's just 'doctor' over here, but please, call me Imran," he replied. "What brings you both to our humble hospital?"

Graham and Gwen exchanged a brief glance before starting their cover story.

Gwen noticed growing agitation in Imran's eyes as they darted between them and the corridor behind them. He wasn't interested. He shifted from one foot to the other, and the moment he found an excuse to leave, he practically bolted. They watched him go.

Beside her, Graham's disappointment was

palpable. Gwen found herself wondering what kind of man Imran had been at medical school.

"I'm afraid Imran's not the man he once was," said Ranil. His words confirmed that Imran had changed, and not for the better. "He spends a lot of time with the bigwigs these days because of his groundbreaking research. His work attracts sponsorship, which has inflated his self-importance, although like every hospital, we need the money."

"He was always bright," said Graham, his voice flat.

Ranil took his arm. "Come, my office is down here. We can stop for a coffee."

11

Sitting in Ranil's expansive office with a mug of hot coffee in his hand, Graham felt the shock of being rebuffed by an old college friend dissolve. He and Imran had never been close, but the man had been almost hostile and certainly rude. It was a sad fact of life that some people changed for the worse. Ranil, on the other hand, was the same outgoing, warm-hearted person he had shared his hopes and dreams with. Ranil had married his childhood sweetheart and had three grown-up children and six grandchildren. He was showing Gwen framed photos that sat proudly on his desk.

"I was sorry about your wife, Graham. We all were."

Graham's wife had died of cancer, which had

wrenched his heart in two. He had vowed never to marry again because he never wanted to experience that pain again. But sometimes...

"What are the kids up to these days?"

Graham was pulled from his musings. He and his wife had two daughters before having two sons. "The two boys are settled in Melbourne with wives of their own. You know I'm a grandfather?"

Ranil smiled happily. "I was just showing Gwen photos of my grandchildren. I think you said your daughter was a lawyer in London. What about your other daughter?"

Graham felt his heart grow heavy, and a frown formed on his face. His youngest daughter, Carol, had felt her mother's loss deeply and had grown increasingly distant from the rest of the family. If he was honest, he didn't know how she was. It had been months since they had spoken because every time she telephoned, the chip on her shoulder seemed to have grown. Her calls usually ended abruptly with the excuse that she was losing her phone signal. "She's backpacking through South America."

Ranil took the hint, and Gwen shot him an empathetic look. Graham had discussed the situation with Gwen, who reassured him that Carol would come back when she was ready. For now, he sent a monthly allowance to her bank account and kept tabs on withdrawals. At least the withdrawals told him she was safe.

"What do your children do?" Graham was thankful when Gwen diverted the conversation away.

"My oldest, like Graham's youngest son, is a doctor, but he works in Trincomalee, a beautiful paradise on the east side of the island. We have a family get-together at his home every year. He doesn't have any children yet, although we hope that someday he and his wife will. My youngest son is a professor at Colombo University. These are his children." Ranil picked up the framed photo of a happy couple with four children and showed it to Graham, having already shown it to Gwen. "And my daughter is a stay-at-home mum – a rarity in Sri Lanka these days. I expect it will change when they have their second child, but for now, she's happy. She trained as a doctor but didn't practice. They live on the outskirts of Colombo, and her husband is a banker. What about you, Gwen?"

"It's just me so far. Never met the right fella."

Graham noticed Gwen break eye contact. He was well aware of the rumour mill that Gwen had been in love with one of Graham's counterparts on another ship and that they had had an affair. The medic had said he was getting divorced, but it all turned out to be a lie, so Gwen had left and joined the *Coral Queen*.

The latter was something Graham would always be grateful for, but he was sorry she had experienced the former.

Ranil gave her an encouraging nod. "An attractive woman like you won't be alone forever. Sometimes what we need most is right in front of our eyes."

Gwen flushed, her light green eyes pretending to scrutinise another photo on Ranil's desk. He found her humility when people complimented her reassuring. She had no idea just how attractive she was, always more focused on those around her than on herself. Her compassion mixed with competence did her credit. Sometimes Graham found it hard to take his eyes off her, she wore her brown hair in a classic bob with blonde streaks perfectly suiting her smooth face. Ranil gave Graham a wink, pulling him from his musings.

Before his old friend dropped any further hints that might be less subtle, Graham felt it was time to explore the email where Ranil had shared his constant battle with patients suffering from drug addiction. He'd mentioned patients dying from overdoses and medical resources being in demand to combat the use of illicit drugs.

Gwen picked up a book on the very topic before she turned to Ranil. "Graham mentioned Colombo has a problem with drug gangs. That must be hard."

"It's true." Ranil's tone turned sombre as he took a sip of coffee. "It's always been a troublesome issue to control, not just in Colombo, but for all of Asia. Things are worse than ever now. It's a very lucrative business, meaning we simply don't know who is involved and who isn't. Opiates frequently go missing from our pharmacy and from ward stocks despite all the safety measures being put in place."

"Is there not a paper trail from your records?" Graham asked.

"Records can be altered, my friend. We have to depend on whistleblowers, but they have a habit of going missing."

"Have you reported this to the authorities?" Gwen asked.

"Of course," Ranil replied, his jaw set. "But progress is slow. The problem is so widespread and deeply ingrained in the system. Recently, a porter came to me and confessed he had become involved in theft and had become an addict. I told him to report it, and the poor man was fired for his trouble. Easier to shoot the messenger, as you would say. Now he's had one of his kidneys removed. If his liver fails... Well..."

Gwen gave Graham a nod, confirming the story of the man Sim, whom she had met on the surgical ward. "Are you suggesting someone in your hospital had him fired?" Graham asked.

"I know they did, but he was an addict and had access to drugs, so they had genuine reasons to sack him. We need concrete evidence before we can take any meaningful action. And when I say we... I mean the handful of us who are interested in dealing with this issue. Even then..." Ranil splayed his hands, palms up.

Graham hated to see his friend put in this position when he knew all he wanted to do was treat and heal the sick. He leaned forward, lowering his voice even though they were the only three in the room with the door closed. "Do you think there is high-level corruption involved? Someone on the hospital payroll who can control the flow of drugs and interfere with any investigation?"

Ranil frowned. "It's not out of the question. Corruption has a way of seeping into Colombo society."

"Even inside the hospital?" Gwen asked.

"Especially here. Remember, we are an easy target, and the stakes are high. These people get rich from creating and enhancing human misery. They don't care about the consequences. No-one is immune to temptation. Many drugs went missing yesterday, along with one of our pharmacists. A devout man who I would have sworn was incorruptible."

Graham raked a hand through his hair, resisting an overwhelming urge to tell his friend that his trust in the deceased Davi was not misplaced. He didn't dare involve Ranil in their dangerous mission, so he held his peace, other than saying, "There might be an innocent explanation for the coincidence."

Gwen offered a look of sympathy and support. It was funny how she could read him.

"I hope there is, Graham; otherwise, my trust radar is off. Still, it's not all bad. We are making excellent advances in medical care, and our organ transplant programme has come about largely because of the money invested by Imran's supporters and pharmaceutical companies."

Could Imran be involved? When in London, Imran had been a strict Muslim, which would normally exclude him from involvement in what was going on here. But people changed, and Ranil had pointed out that Imran was now friends with influential people, and judging by their meeting, he had indeed changed. Was it from arrogance or corruption? He would discuss the matter with Gwen later.

Ranil appeared happy the subject had changed to more positive events, and they discussed his work at the hospital in more depth.

"What about you, Graham? I know I teased you earlier, but it can't be easy being responsible for the rich and privileged on a cruise ship."

"Don't believe everything you read in the papers, Ranil. People from all walks of life take cruises nowadays, and we're also responsible for the health of around two thousand crew members at any one time. Most of them come from poorer countries and send money home to support their families. In fact, we have a large Indian contingent and a small Sri Lankan pool of workers. Below deck, we're like the United Nations."

"I hadn't thought about the crew. Tell me more about your work."

"Well, in terms of turnover, it's like yours. We can accommodate three thousand passengers – more when families share rooms – who board at varying intervals from one to two weeks mostly, but there are those who join us for longer periods."

"World cruises," said Gwen. "A passenger admitted to your surgical ward yesterday for an appendicectomy is one such cruiser."

"Most of our passengers are healthy, but some have long-term conditions that are under control. We even have a few who board for end-of-life care."

"Really?"

"They usually bring private nurses to accompany

them, but Graham is still responsible for the oversight," Gwen added.

"Can you operate?"

"Yes, when necessary, and we have an intensive care bed with a ventilator. Gwen and the other nurses are excellent with accidents and emergencies, and our junior doctor also has a lot of experience. We've dealt with just about every emergency you can name, as well as minor ailments, and of course, the odd infectious outbreak."

"Ah, the dreaded norovirus," said Ranil. "We get that too."

Gwen interjected again. "If Graham feels a passenger's condition is too serious to wait until we dock, we can head to the nearest port, speed up the ship, or call for help."

"Such as?"

"Air ambulance if it's serious enough, or boat ambulance for things like broken limbs. Minor bone fractures we can X-ray and plaster ourselves, but those that need surgery we refer on."

"What about the crew? What are you dealing with there?" Ranil asked.

"Anything from minor illnesses to major accidents. But to be honest, a lot of what we deal with results from brawls, a penalty for cheap alcohol," Graham said, sighing. If it was up to him, he'd impose an alcohol limit, but the crew worked long shifts and deserved to enjoy themselves during their downtime like everyone else in the world. Graham didn't mention murder, sexual assault, and domestic violence among passengers mostly, and crew occasionally.

Gwen added, "We're about the size of a village or a small town, with some regulars – our crew – and a lot of visitors – the passengers. We deal with all the health troubles that brings, and our security team handles anything involving crime."

"Maybe if I tire of being a hospital consultant, and my wife would move away from her grandchildren, I should try it," said Ranil, smiling. "I'd have to update my knowledge on accident and emergency, though, because I'm a little rusty there."

"Any cruise line would be lucky to have you, Ranil, but I suspect you're as tied to your family as your wife is," said Graham.

Ranil's bleep went off. He looked at it and shot an apologetic look their way.

"We've kept you too long," said Graham. "Would it be okay if Gwen and I stop by your pharmacy and look around?"

A flicker of hesitation flashed through Ranil's eyes before he shrugged. "Why not? I'll call them now, and then I'm needed on the wards. Perhaps we could have dinner while you're in town?"

"We'd love that," said Gwen.

"I'll call you to arrange something," said Ranil. "I'm sure I've got your number in my phone. I don't carry it around with me, it's enough carrying a bleep."

Graham empathised. "I know what you mean. We carry radios for direct contact but we also have a coded announcement system.

"I look forward to hearing more about that over dinner," said Ranil before giving them directions to the hospital pharmacy. He assured them the head pharmacist would give them a tour.

12

Gwen and Graham joined a queue of people waiting for prescriptions to be dispensed. This gave Gwen time to observe the activity behind the glass panel. The pharmacy mirrored the rest of the hospital, bustling with frenetic movement; pharmacy technicians and pharmacists flitted between shelves, their white coats fluttering like the wings of doves.

As their turn came to speak through a space in the glass-fronted desk, Gwen tried to sound friendly. "Hello, I'm Gwen Sumner, and this is Dr Graham Bentley. We've just been with Dr Ranil Fernando. I believe you're expecting us." The man at the desk appeared confused and shouted in Sinhalese to the person in a lab coat behind him, who called to someone else out of sight.

A white woman wearing a white lab coat stepped forward and spoke to the man at reception, who pressed a buzzer.

"Push the door to your left," she said.

Gwen did as instructed, and before long, they were inside the secure part of the pharmacy, where all the activity was taking place.

"Elize Frazier, pleased to meet you." Gwen didn't get the impression the tight lipped woman was pleased at all. "Ranil telephoned, apparently you would like a tour." She sighed, almost rolling her eyes in the process. "Come this way. A lot of the staff here don't speak English. The pharmacists do, of course, but they're mostly European-educated."

Graham tried to shake hands with Elize, but she was already leading them through the stocked aisles into an office. She thrust a book towards them. "Sign in, please."

Gwen was happy to see they kept a record of visitors to the pharmacy, although, as Ranil had pointed out, records can be altered.

"Is that a South African accent I detect?" Graham asked after signing.

"Johannesburg. You're English, I take it?"

"I am. Gwen's Australian."

While Graham kept Elize talking, Gwen signed the book, scanning the list of names. A recent visitor's signature caught her eye. It appeared DI Rohan de Silva had been there the evening before.

"Is the pharmacy twenty-four hours?" Gwen asked as Elize snatched the visitor book from her hands and placed it back on the minimalist desk.

Gwen herself liked order, and if the woman weren't so curt, she would have taken to her. They were about the same age.

"I don't have much time, but I'll show you around," Elize said, her tone brisk. "In answer to your question, we offer twenty-four-hour cover. The wards hold some prescribing stock, but sometimes they need something not so readily available."

Observing the staff around them, Gwen felt a pang of sympathy. Elize's frosty demeanour seemed to create a chilly atmosphere in the pharmacy. The staff shied away from her, their movements cautious, as if navigating a minefield. It appeared Gwen wasn't the only one finding the manager's manner off-putting.

Graham used his diplomatic skills to keep Elize occupied with questions while Gwen took the time to observe the staff more closely. It was like watching an assembly line in a factory. Each worker collected medicines, filled bottles, and marked off check-sheets in a robotic fashion. Among the sea of lab coats, one man caught Gwen's attention. There was a certain familiarity in his features that tugged at her memory. He resembled Tiffany's murdered friend, Davi. Gwen wondered if he was a relative. She tried to approach him to check the name badge, offering a friendly hello. He looked drawn and weary.

"This way," Elize called, her voice sharp enough to cut glass. "Please don't distract the staff. They need to concentrate."

"Of course," said Gwen. "Sorry." But she wasn't sorry; she was concerned.

Graham exchanged a glance with Gwen, who rolled her eyes. Elize was robotic in her replies until Graham asked her about her own role, at which point she raised her head with pride. "I manage a team of thirty: seven pharmacists, eighteen technicians, and five runners."

"That must be quite a responsibility," said Gwen, following Graham's lead. "How do you keep track of everything?"

"We have a rigorous system in place. I make sure of that. Before I came, drugs were all over the place. Now we store them alphabetically, and every tablet, powder, cream, and ampoule is audited, from delivery to dispensing."

I wonder how things go missing then? Gwen thought to herself.

"We do the same on board the *Coral Queen*," she said. "But it's nothing like this scale."

Elize was positively preening now. "This is the biggest hospital in Sri Lanka, so yes, it takes a lot of work. My predecessor let things slip, so the hospital board appointed me. Dr Bentley mentioned you are Australian."

"Born and bred," said Gwen. "I trained in Melbourne and travelled a bit before joining the cruise line."

"I have a brother in Adelaide. Are you staying long?"

"Maybe a week or two while the ship undergoes some repairs," said Gwen, sensing they were breaking down Elize's barriers. "If you like, we could meet for coffee? We don't know the city at all."

"That would be doable, I suppose." Elize hesitated.

Gwen caught sight of a figure approaching them from across the pharmacy. The woman's stride was confident, almost predatory – a lioness stalking her prey.

The woman stopped in front of them, raising a quizzical eyebrow at Elize. "This is Mrs Priya Mendis," said Elize. "Mrs Mendis is head of the board of directors and a government minister."

"Good afternoon." Priya Mendis's dark eyes

narrowed as they turned on Graham and Gwen. "Visitors?"

"Yes," Graham began, feigning innocence. "We're medics from the *Coral Queen* cruise ship. I trained with Dr Ranil Fernando many years ago."

"I see. I wasn't aware of any official visits taking place," Priya Mendis said, her voice slightly less stern. Gwen could feel the weight of her scrutiny as the woman studied them both.

"It was a spontaneous arrangement. I paid a visit to my old friend, but he got called away, and being in the same profession, we couldn't resist seeing how the biggest and best hospital in Colombo operates."

Mendis smiled. "We do our best. Where is Dr Fernando now?"

"He was called away," repeated Gwen. "And Ms Frazier has been good enough to show us around the pharmacy."

"Are you impressed by what you see?" Mendis asked.

Gwen forced a bright smile. "Very. It's not every day we get to visit such a beautiful country. Your pharmacy is admirable. Elize was telling us about your audit trail."

"I'm pleased to hear it, but we don't normally allow people to wander around our hospital, especially its pharmacy." At this point, Priya Mendis glared at Elize.

"Then we won't take up any more of Elize's time," said Graham. "Thank you for showing us around." Graham shook Elize's hand this time.

"Sorry if we got you into trouble," said Gwen.

"Elize's not in trouble," said Priya Mendis. "But Dr Fernando might be." Priya Mendis forced a laugh, but Gwen got the impression she wasn't joking.

"Thanks again," said Graham. "Should we sign out?"

"No need for––"

"Yes. Follow me."

Clearly, Elize would tolerate interference to a point, but not when it came to running her department. Gwen chuckled inwardly.

"Of course," Mrs Mendis said, her tone as cold as ice.

Gwen slipped Elize her card. "That's my mobile number if you want to get a coffee sometime," she whispered.

After they had signed their exit time in the visitor's book, Mrs Mendis was waiting for them. "I'll see you out."

It wasn't a request, so Gwen and Graham followed the official, who marched them from the pharmacy to the hospital entrance. "Enjoy the rest of your visit to

Colombo," she said before spinning on her heels, leaving Gwen and Graham rooted to the spot.

As they watched the woman disappear back inside the hospital, Gwen and Graham laughed. "That's us told," Gwen said.

"I felt like a naughty schoolboy."

"Let's get out of here," Gwen said, feeling more serious. "I reckon Priya Mendis will put paid to any impromptu tours from now on."

"We've still got the ace card up our sleeve, remember?"

"Oh yes. Ben Thompson. We forgot to mention him."

"Perhaps it's for the best. I wouldn't want to put him on Priya Mendis's radar."

"Good point."

It was just after six o'clock when they left the hospital grounds, and the sun was dipping below the horizon, casting a warm glow across the bustling streets of Colombo. The Christmas decorations were lit up, and an enormous, decorated Christmas tree stood proudly in the modern part of the town centre. The air was thick with the mixed scent of spices and exhaust fumes, blending together in the smog.

"Where to now?" Gwen asked.

"Dinner. Then I'll see you back to the YMCA and head back to the *Coral Queen*," said Graham.

13

Scents of spices and exhaust fumes hung in the evening air. Gwen had to resist the urge to link her arm with Graham's as they wandered through the bustling Colombo town centre. Evening activities were well underway as tourists, locals and traders mingled in close proximity. Christmas lights twinkled incongruously against the tropical night sky, strung between colonial buildings. Ceiling fans whirred in open-air bars. The streets teemed with tourists in sundresses and locals in business suits heading home. Tuk-tuks and motorcycles wove expertly through the traffic, their horns adding to the city's noise. They passed the entrance to a huge shopping centre housing European and internationally known stores. Outside, young professionals gathered for drinks, their laughter carried on the humid breeze. There was the familiar and the unfamiliar all around them. Gwen was at odds with her feelings, acutely aware of Graham's presence yet reluctant to cross the professional relationship they had nurtured. Not to mention that one shouldn't get distracted by someone they're investigating murder with, no matter how charming their smile is in the glow of the street lamps.

"What about this place?" Graham raised his voice to be heard above the noise.

Several locals were eating inside a restaurant alongside tourists. "If it's good enough for the locals," she replied.

Graham stepped back to allow her to enter first. He was a throwback to a previous generation with his manners. Never superior, but always respectful. She entered the busy restaurant.

The suited man looked past Gwen. "Do you have a booking, sir?"

Gwen sighed. Another throwback, but more condescending.

"No. We're new to Colombo. Can you fit us in with a table for two?"

"One moment, sir." The man turned and spoke to someone who was clearly his boss before addressing Graham again, as though Gwen was invisible. "We have a table, sir. There's usually a dress code…" he shot a disapproving look in Gwen's direction. She was wearing knee-length cotton shorts and a purple t-shirt, having been out for most of the day. Graham, however, was wearing a suit as he always did, although his jacket hung over his arm. "But as you're new to our wonderful city, we'll make an exception. Name, please?"

"Graham Bentley."

Gwen was pleased he hadn't given her name. They hadn't discussed whether they should use pseudonyms while in Colombo, but as they weren't on anyone's radar, it should be fine to use his.

A waiter approached them. "Follow me, please, sir."

Gwen was growing more irritated by the second. She hoped they served good food to make up for the patriarchal attitude. They were shown to a table where one glance at the menu told Gwen this wasn't an average Sri Lankan restaurant. Glancing around the room, she noticed a few people giving her looks, muttering to each other before turning back to their food. She was pleased to be seated.

"Sorry about that. I should have noticed," said Graham. "I think you look perfect, by the way."

Was he teasing, or was there genuine warmth in

his eyes? "They'll get over it. I'm sure they've seen worse."

Graham scanned the wine menu. "Are you happy with a Riesling? It says here it pairs well with spicy food."

"Sounds good to me," she replied. "And a bottle of mineral water. I'm parched."

"Good idea."

After Graham ordered a bottle of German Riesling and two bottles of water, Gwen gazed through the window. They were sitting on the side of the restaurant overlooking a public park. She could see the greenery illuminated by fluorescent lights. Graham perused the menu.

The scent of spices coming from the kitchen made her feel hungry, so she scanned the menu herself, pleased it was in English and Sinhalese. A waiter came to take their order.

Gwen ordered a chicken curry with rice, and Graham opted for a crab curry. The waiter suggested papadams and dips as an appetiser, and they accepted.

Once the waiter left with their order, Graham lowered his voice. "We'll need to keep our heads down at the National after today. I'm not sure about that woman, Priya Mendis."

"I wouldn't be surprised if she was involved. She seemed eager to get rid of us."

"Unless she's protecting the pharmacy from strangers who might be dealers. What did you make of Elize?"

"I can't see her being involved, but how they circumvent her system is a mystery. Guess whose name was in the visitor book?"

"Ah, I was hoping you'd pick something up there. Was it the detective?"

"The very one. He'd been there the night before. That's why I asked about the opening hours."

"I felt bad not being able to exonerate the pharmacist in Ranil's eyes, but I don't want him to get caught up in this. Not until we have evidence."

"If we'd been given the opportunity, it would have been useful to find out whether any of the pharmacy staff would mention him." Gwen looked out of the window again and then back at Graham. "At least we have a good cover story for going to the hospital and who we are. Anyone checking up will discover we are exactly who we say we are."

Graham appeared to relax. "Very true."

A waiter arrived with the wine and water. He poured water into glasses and then opened the wine, pouring a small amount into a glass for Graham to savour. Many wine-tasting courses on board the *Coral Queen* seemed to have paid off. Graham was always regaling the team with information about wines from various vineyards. After going through his ritual of examining, swirling, sniffing, and tasting, he gave the waiter a nod.

With glasses full, Gwen took a sip. "Not half bad," she said, grinning.

Graham chuckled.

Gwen wondered if he planned to buy a vineyard when he retired, but the thought of him retiring made her uneasy.

They chatted easily while starters were served, followed by the main courses. The curry was rich in flavour, and they ate in comfortable silence, with the occasional conversation about cruise ship life. Gwen would have liked to ask him about his daughter, Carol. He had told her in the past that he worried about her, but other than knowing Carol had chosen to escape responsibility through travel, she knew little more. Graham often spoke about his sons; the eldest was a dentist with two daughters, and the youngest a doctor. She had met them and their families when they joined the *Coral Queen* in Melbourne during an Australasian cruise. Sometimes, when they docked in Southampton, Graham went to London to visit his eldest daughter, Helen, whom Gwen hadn't met.

"This has got to be one of the best curries I've ever tasted," Gwen said.

"This one's not so bad either. It's good to see you relaxing, Gwen. This was supposed to be your holiday."

As the wine filtered through and the meal was ending, Gwen relaxed. "It's a good thing we never know what life's going to throw at us, isn't it?"

Graham lowered his voice again. "What are the chances of us finding someone in authority who could help us?"

"I would suggest they are pretty low," Gwen replied, frowning.

"Perhaps Jack has some local police contacts. I could ask him."

"But even if he does, we can't be certain they would be trustworthy. If we can uncover the truth about the drug problems Ranil mentioned, we might stand a chance."

"Perhaps, but I can't see how we can get any more information than what he told us," Graham said, his brow furrowed in concentration. "Or how we can find out without exposing ourselves?"

Gwen polished off the last mouthful of her delicious chicken curry and placed her knife and fork on her plate. She took another sip of wine. "The only lead we have so far is Sim. We'll have to go back to the hospital tomorrow to see Ben Thompson."

"You're right, of course."

"I gave Elize my card and suggested coffee, but I can't see her contacting me."

"You never know. She might be less fierce when she's out of that place. I guess she has a lot on her plate."

The waiter topped up both their glasses with the remains of the bottle, and Gwen held up her glass. "Then we have a plan. We will not let these criminals win, Graham. For Tiffany's sake."

"I'll drink to that," he said, his eyes meeting hers. His face was flushed. Was it from the alcohol?

"This stuff's strong. It's going to my head," Gwen said.

An unexpected presence at their table brought their calm conversation to an end. At first, Gwen thought it was the waiter, but when she looked up, she had to stop herself from gasping.

"Good evening. I'm Detective Inspector Rohan de Silva," his stern expression belied an undercurrent of malice.

Graham showed no sign of stress. Thanks to years dealing with emergencies, he was used to the unexpected and knew how to hide his feelings. He stood up, shaking the detective's hand.

"Dr Graham Bentley and Sister Gwen Sumner from the *Coral Queen*. I hope we haven't broken any laws, Inspector?"

The inspector forced a smile. "I saw you at the hospital earlier." His cold eyes fixed on Gwen's. "I never forget a face."

"I vaguely remember," said Gwen, trying to sound calmer than she felt.

"Sister Sumner was visiting a patient on Ward 17, I believe."

"Yes. Mr Thompson," said Gwen. "As Graham mentioned, we're from the *Coral Queen* cruise ship. Mr Thompson fell ill yesterday and had his appendix removed at the impressive hospital."

"Very good of you to pay him a visit. That's dedication for you." His derision was unmistakable.

"We're nothing if not dedicated, Inspector de Silva," said Graham. "In fact, we were just discussing whether I should visit him tomorrow. The staff would like to discharge him back to our care once he's ready, and Gwen tells me his daughter is keen for that to happen."

"Is that so?" de Silva raised an eyebrow, scrutinising them both with piercing eyes. "Have you ever visited our hospital, Dr Bentley?"

Gwen had the impression de Silva knew all about their tour of the hospital, and his presence in the restaurant wasn't a coincidence. She jumped in before Graham could answer.

"Graham trained with one of the consultants who works there – two of them, actually."

"Yes. Ranil Fernando offered to give me a tour while we are laid up for repairs. I met Gwen for lunch at the hospital today, and then we caught up with him," Graham added.

"Yes, I heard about the tour."

He had been looking into them. Gwen tried to control her breathing and looked de Silva in the eye. "Wow! I would have thought you had more on your plate than a couple of foreign tourists visiting a patient and an old friend."

de Silva appeared surprised. He brushed imaginary fluff from the sleeve of his jacket.

"Is there anything else we can do for you, Inspector?" Graham asked, retaking his seat. "Would you like to join us? We've eaten already, but you'd be welcome to join us for coffee."

"No, thank you. As Sister Sumner says, I'm a busy man. Is that an Australian accent?" de Silva's eyes narrowed as he stared at Gwen.

"Yes, it is, but it's been many years since I lived in Australia."

"There are a few Australians working at the National. Perhaps you might know them?"

Gwen felt her heart pounding. Was this man just fishing, or had he checked on Tiffany's connections? No. He couldn't have done that already. "I don't think so. Not anyone I've kept in touch with, or I'd look them up. Australia is a big country."

She knew well that at least three people in Tiffany's condo had seen her but was certain de Silva wouldn't have had time to question the building's residents. Not without declaring a body had been found.

"Excuse my interrupting your dinner. Please enjoy the rest of your evening." He made a move to leave before turning back. "Will you be staying in Colombo long?"

"We're not sure," said Gwen. "The ship's undergoing repairs."

"Well, be careful. Colombo can be a dangerous place."

"Thanks for the warning, inspector. Are you dining here tonight?" Graham asked.

"No," he said, turning on his heels and heading out of the restaurant.

"What was that all about?" Gwen asked.

"I think Rohan de Silva is worried. He knows your cousin is not in Colombo, and he's checking us out; weighing up his options."

"How long before he discovers she's my cousin?"

"I don't know. Are you sure you don't want to come back to the ship? What if he has you followed?"

Gwen shook her head. "He'd need a lot of corrupt officers to do that. I think he was just unsettled seeing me on the ward and hearing about our tour. Hopefully, he's just checking up."

"So, how did he find us this evening?"

Gwen held her palms out. "That, I don't know. He could have called around restaurants."

"Maybe," Graham murmured. "I don't like this development. Let's get out of here and go to the Hilton. Once I'm satisfied we're not being followed, we'll call Tiffany."

"Okay," Gwen said.

Graham asked for the bill and paid with a credit card.

Gwen had been looking behind them as they made their way out of the restaurant. Rohan de Silva had unnerved her. It didn't help to know how dangerous the man was.

14

Graham and Gwen walked to the Hilton, and Graham was confident they hadn't been followed. He hoped that the detective inspector would soon forget about them and return to his shady deeds. Not long after Gwen ordered, two coffees were placed on their table, Graham's phone rang. Gwen appeared tense as the ringtone jolted them from their thoughts. He looked at the screen.

"It's Ranil," he said to Gwen, tapping to answer. "Hello, Ranil."

"Hi Graham. It was great to see you today."

"You too. Are you calling to arrange that dinner date?"

"Yes and no. Listen, I just wanted to warn you

about a woman called Priya Mendis. I believe you met her today."

"We did. She turned up when we were visiting the pharmacy. Sorry if we got you into trouble."

"You didn't, but she's a powerful woman, and she wasn't happy. She's since sent a memo to all staff that foreigners are not allowed to tour the facilities. She's citing concerns that they might be criminals because of the drug thefts issue. I guess she has a point, but I reassured her you and I go way back. She said there would be no exceptions. I'm sorry."

"No problem. We enjoyed the tour, but it wouldn't be something we'd repeat. Thanks for letting me know," Graham replied. "I doubt we'll see her again, but if we do, we'll keep our distance." Graham forced a laugh, trying to sound more relaxed than he felt. He considered mentioning how a DI had tracked them down to a restaurant but opted not to involve Ranil in anything that might put him at risk.

"Now, about that dinner. I know a good place that's off the tourist trail, which serves amazing Asian cuisine."

"Sounds perfect," said Graham. "When?"

"Would the day after tomorrow suit? Say eight o'clock."

"Okay. And if you're available before dinner, I'll give you a tour of the *Coral Queen*."

Ranil's voice sounded eager as he replied. "I'd love that."

"Could you meet me at around five-thirty? I'll make sure there's a visitor's pass waiting for you at the entrance to the dock. They'll call me, and I'll take you through security."

"I can't wait," said Ranil.

"One good turn deserves another. I'll let Gwen know about dinner. Looking forward to it."

After ending the call, Graham told Gwen about the plan before adding, "I'm pretty sure Priya Mendis has revealed her involvement. She's put out a memo banning foreign tours of the hospital. According to Ranil, she claims she wants to protect the hospital from drug gangs."

"Things are going from bad to worse," Gwen replied. "Do you think she suspects us?"

"Not necessarily. I believe she spoke to Ranil and de Silva, but Ranil has confirmed everything we've said. de Silva obviously did his homework about the *Coral Queen's* extended stay and wanted to check us out. He must be satisfied with what he's heard. He'll forget about us and focus on getting that body out of Tiffany's condo and go back to his criminal ways."

"Either way, he'll be looking for Tiff."

"Who is on holiday. Thankfully, she gave no reason to her manager, and when de Silva makes enquiries, if he hasn't already, he'll assume she's having a good time in Mumbai."

Gwen looked less than assured as she replied, "But how do we carry on with people on the lookout for us?"

"By being smarter than them," Graham said. "We still have Mr Thompson. And I suggest that when we visit tomorrow, we expedite his return to the ship, whether he's gathered any information from Sim or not."

"I agree with you there. We don't want to put him at risk."

"When I see Janet later, I'll tell her about the discharge plan so she doesn't sound surprised if the ward contacts the ship."

"Good. Let's use a landline to call Tiffany and Nalini before you head back to the ship." Gwen had made it clear she didn't want Graham to be seen at the YMCA in case it raised questions about her tourist status.

Nalini answered on the third ring. "Hello?"

"Nalini, it's Graham."

"Good evening. How are your investigations going?"

"We've made some progress," said Graham. "Is everything okay there?"

"All good. Tiffany has been most helpful. We've

been putting up Christmas decorations. I haven't bothered since Ramesh died, but I thought it would be nice to cheer the place up a little."

And keep Tiffany occupied, no doubt, thought Graham. "That's a marvellous idea."

"I won't waste your time, Graham, because it's late. Here's Tiffany. Please don't worry about her. This place is quiet."

"Hi Graham. Is Gwen okay?"

"She is. She's with me now. We've been drinking coffee." Gwen smiled but Graham recognised the tension in her face. "We're fine. Gwen's staying at the YMCA like you suggested. We've just been out for dinner and thought we'd call from the Hilton before I head back to the ship. We're using the hotel landline." Gwen hadn't wanted either of them to use their phones in case de Silva was tracking their calls, which he thought was unlikely.

"Did you find anything out?"

"I can't talk for long." Graham hoped that would be enough to deflect any direct questioning. "We met my old friend, Dr Ranil Fernando, and managed a tour of the hospital, which was interesting and enlightening, but so far we've got little to go on."

"It sounds like you're making progress. Look, tell Gwen I've been racking my brains all day and there's a guy in the police force I met twice. He's honest."

"How did you meet him?"

"Through a nurse friend, Anjali. He's her cousin. She was going on a first date and wanted to keep it low-key, so she invited me and Arjun. If you want someone on the inside, he's your man. He's a devout Buddhist."

"Let Gwen have his details, and we'll try to contact him. Thanks for that. Now rest up and don't worry. Here's Gwen for a quick word."

Graham watched as Gwen scribbled down the name of the policeman on a pad and pushed it inside her handbag. It was obvious Tiffany was asking Gwen the same questions she'd asked him because Gwen gave the same answers. Before saying goodbye, Gwen asked to speak to Nalini. Graham listened to Gwen thanking Nalini again for her help before mentioning the exit plan they had discussed earlier. When she ended the call, he looked at her.

"She couldn't say much, but reading between the lines, I don't think Tiff is ready to leave Sri Lanka just yet. Sounds like they're having fun, though."

"Perhaps they'll help each other. Nalini and Ramesh were close. It can't have been easy for her since he died."

"She gave me the name of the man she believes is a good cop. She mentioned him to you."

"Yes. We might need to contact him. But it's

getting late. Are you sure you don't want me to escort you back to your digs?"

"Positive. I don't want to look anything other than a tourist. Why do you think I'm dressed like this?"

"To annoy posh hotel waiters," he said, laughing.

Gwen chuckled. "You can take me as far as the end of the road. It's best if I keep up with the tourist thing."

Graham walked with Gwen, again checking they weren't being followed. They weren't. For now, de Silva had swallowed their story. Just before they parted, he felt an overwhelming urge to pull her into his arms. What was the matter with him?

"Meet you tomorrow outside the hospital," she said.

Not trusting himself to speak, he nodded. He watched Gwen walk away with an ache in his heart. Putting it down to concern for her safety, Graham waited until she was out of sight before heading back to the ship, confused and a little frightened. Was it the responsibility of solving this crime weighing heavily, or something far scarier?

15

Gwen was feeling the stress of the past two days when she reached the entrance to the YMCA. Her heart quickened when her phone rang. Had Graham forgotten something? She reached for her phone and checked the screen; it was an unknown number. Tentatively, she pressed answer.

"Hello?"

"It's Elize Frazier. Is that Gwen Sumner?"

"Hi. Yes, this is me."

"Sorry to call so late, but I was wondering if you wanted to grab that coffee you mentioned, or maybe something stronger?" Elize sounded much chirpier than when they'd met earlier.

Gwen was exhausted and just wanted to get to

bed, but this could be a meeting worth pushing past her tiredness. "Sure. Where do you suggest?"

"I'm at the Sky Lounge. It's a rooftop bar at the Kingsbury Hotel. Do you know it?"

"No, but I'm sure I can find it."

"Where are you?"

"Erm. I was just heading back to the ship, but I can make a detour." Gwen didn't want anyone from the hospital knowing she wasn't sleeping aboard the *Coral Queen*. "I'll see you in a bit."

Gwen debated whether to let Graham know where she was going and who she was meeting, but she didn't want him to worry. Plus, he'd feel obligated to offer to join them. *No. He's got enough on his plate.* There would be several things needing his attention when he got back to the ship, as it was. She opted not to call him and hailed a tuk-tuk on the main road.

After haggling the price down to one she was happy with, she climbed inside.

The cityscape was beautiful, the night lighting up the high-rise buildings. Outside the Kingsbury, an enormous Christmas tree stood beside a stunningly lit rickshaw. As Gwen strolled into the exotic hotel, it buzzed with activity. She took a lift to the tenth floor, having received information from Elize via text. Elize was waiting for her as she exited the lift. Gwen felt underdressed in her shorts. Elize wore a ruby red cocktail dress and looked stunning. Her smile was radiant. Was this really the same woman Gwen and Graham had met that afternoon?

"Hello, Gwen, glad you could come. No Dr Bentley this evening?"

"Alas, he had work to get back to."

"Even better. I see enough doctors during the day." There was a sparkle in Elize's eyes, which Gwen couldn't decipher. Maybe she'd been drinking.

"I would have changed if I'd realised it was a posh restaurant."

"Don't worry about that. I eat here a lot, and I've not long had dinner, so they won't give you any trouble. We can enjoy the spectacular views and have a drink. The cocktails are second to none. You can even have them make a signature cocktail just for you."

That's the coffee out of the window then, thought Gwen. Grateful her head had cleared from the wine she'd had with dinner, she followed the transformed Elize to a window table. "Wow! You were right, the view is stunning." Gwen briefly envisioned her and Graham enjoying dinner for two overlooking the spectacular Colombo skyline but quickly shook the thought from her head.

"Is something the matter?" Elize asked.

"No. Sorry, I was thinking of something else. Thank you for inviting me. It's amazing."

Elize seemed pleased before a faraway look appeared in her dark brown eyes. "This is my favourite place in Colombo, my own carefree space," she said at last. "Let's get a drink."

Gwen scanned the cocktail menu. There was clearly a hefty price to pay for the salubrious atmosphere. "Anything you recommend?"

"The Colombo Ocean Mist is good if you're happy with a vodka base."

"Sounds delicious. The Ocean Mist it is then," said Gwen.

After ordering cocktails, they made polite conversation about the views before Gwen asked, "Do you live near here?"

"Not too far away. I rent a condo about half a mile away. Sorry about your visit being cut short earlier. Priya Mendis can be a pain. You'd think she runs the hospital the way she behaves."

"It wasn't a problem. Our visit was more about Graham catching up with his old friend."

"Ranil Fernando?"

"Yes. But we enjoyed the little of the pharmacy we saw. You've certainly got your work cut out."

"Ranil's a decent sort. The hospital has a lot of

good going on, but it also has its issues, which is probably why Priya chased you away."

"Oh? What sort of issues?" Gwen had to feign a polite level of interest without seeming overly keen, which was hard.

There was a temporary delay in conversation while a waiter brought their cocktails and laid them neatly on the table. "We have a problem with drugs going missing," Elize said simply before taking a sip of her cocktail. "To be honest, if I'd realised the scale of the problem before I started, I might not have taken the job, but I needed the money after..." Elize stared into the night, a sadness on her face.

Gwen knew that look. She'd felt the same pain. This woman was recovering from a broken heart. She sipped her drink and waited for Elize to recover.

Her voice trembled as she began, "I was travelling through Asia with my partner. It all started wonderfully. We'd been to Singapore, then travelled up into Malaysia for a few weeks by the sea, and then on to Thailand. That's when the problems started."

"What happened?"

Elize's hands were shaking. "I hadn't realised Matty had messed with drugs in the past. Wherever we went in Thailand, we were offered drugs. At first, we joked about it, but when he started accepting a little cannabis, I got worried. Before long, he was buying stronger stuff. His personality changed completely, becoming unpredictable; aggressive even. More so when I pleaded with him to stop."

"Did Matty come with you to Sri Lanka?"

"Yes. It was always on our itinerary. The plan was to stop here for a few months, work to build up cash reserves, and then travel on to India and Nepal. Matty showed no interest in getting a job and soon ate through his budget. Then he wanted to start on mine. In a last-ditch attempt to get him to see sense, I told him that unless he stopped wasting money on drugs, he would have to travel alone. It all turned sour. Instead of being the nudge he needed, he was livid; called me many things I won't repeat and stormed out of the condo. By that time, I'd got the job at the hospital. I'm a pharmacist by background. I wonder now if that's the reason he asked me out in the first place. Still, there was no way I was going to allow him to manipulate me into getting him drugs, knowing they would ruin his life... and most likely, mine. That was six months ago."

"Where is he now?"

"According to his phone location, he's back in Bangkok. He doesn't answer my calls, and I've stopped trying. It's been hard because he's genuinely the first man I've ever loved, but now I realise I had a lucky escape."

"And you find yourself in a position where there's another problem with drugs at work."

Elize sighed heavily. "Ironic, isn't it? If I hadn't made some good friends here, I'd head back to Johannesburg. I wouldn't risk travelling on through Asia alone. Others do, but I'm too cautious to take that risk. It turns out there's a decent ex-pat community here in Colombo, and I've made a few friends."

"As you said, it was good you found out about Matty before it was too late."

"Yeah, but I mourn the loss of the person he was – or at least the person I thought he was. When we first met, he was fun and full of life. But he's gone, and I'm here."

"What do you think's happening at work? And do you know who's responsible for the issues?"

"I had my suspicions and reported them to the police. There's a detective who's investigating the theft. Apparently, it was a lot worse before I instigated changes to the way we keep records. Now a pharmacist has disappeared, and DI de Silva says he was the guy stealing drugs. I'm finding that a tough pill to swallow. Davi was strait-laced and trustworthy. In fact, he'd warned me that staff were coming under pressure to take drugs."

Gwen's heart raced, struggling to decide whether

to tell Elize what she knew. An inner voice warned her this could be a ploy from de Silva to find out how much she knew. Everything in her wanted to be honest with Elize and warn her not to trust de Silva, but she couldn't. She had to protect Tiffany. "I find it's usually best to trust your instincts. Who did you think was responsible?"

"I was leaning towards Priya Mendis being involved somewhere along the line. There was a hospital porter who stole drugs, and he told one of my pharmacy technicians her office covered the corruption up."

"Blimey. What about the detective inspector? Do you trust him?"

Elize pinched the bridge of her nose. "I did until Davi disappeared. Davi was frightened of him, which could mean he was worried about being found out, or that the DI is involved."

"What does your gut tell you?"

Elize blew out a breath, making her lips bubble. "Before what happened with Matty, I'd have said Davi was a good guy, but now I no longer trust my judgement. If he's innocent, why would he disappear?"

"Good question," said Gwen.

"The only thing I'm confused about is that yesterday when Davi didn't turn up for work, I checked all the stock myself. Then, this morning, opiates were missing. de Silva visited the pharmacy last night..." Elize shrugged, "...it's hard to believe he could be involved. He seemed so keen to find out what was going on."

Gwen could well believe it. "What if he had an ulterior motive?"

"I haven't wanted to go down that road because if I do, I wouldn't know which way to turn. If Priya is involved, and now the detective... Well... Sorry. I didn't mean to offload on you, but with you being a senior nurse, I thought you might understand."

"We've had our share of problems on board ship, but nothing on the same scale. It's usually passengers sneaking on stuff for their own use, or crew trying to earn a fast buck. We do random drug tests on all the crew. I'd love to help you, but I'm not sure there's anything I can do," said Gwen cautiously.

"Do you think Graham... Dr Bentley could mention my concerns to Ranil?"

"Now that, we can do. Graham's giving him a tour of the ship the day after tomorrow, and then we're going out for dinner. Why don't you join him for the tour? I can't invite you to dinner because that was Ranil's invite, not ours."

Elize visibly relaxed. "I'd love to. Whether or not you can help, I'd love to see what you do on board."

"That's settled then. Ranil's arriving at five-thirty. I'll let Graham know and arrange for you to have a guest pass." Gwen finished her drink. "I'd better get back before anyone misses me."

"I'll stick around and admire the view for a bit longer. See you the day after tomorrow."

16

Gwen met Graham just outside the main entrance to the hospital grounds. It was another warm day, and she was feeling upbeat after her conversation with Elize the evening before.

"Before we go inside, I've got something to tell you." Gwen led Graham to a bench where they could sit beneath a palm tree.

"Did something happen? Don't tell me your cover at the YMCA is blown."

"No, nothing like that. On the way back last night, I got a call from Elize Frazier."

"The frosty pharmacist?"

"Yes, but she's much nicer off duty than on. She's got a lot on her mind."

"Why didn't you tell me? It could have been a trap."

"It's okay. We met in a very public place. It was a Sky Lounge at the top of the Kingsbury Hotel. Magnificent views; you and I should..."

Graham grinned. "I'd love to see it, maybe tonight. But what did she want?"

Gwen relaxed, pleased her presumption had not offended him. "I think she wanted to offload on someone outside of work, but still in the profession. The fact is, she opened up about drugs being stolen from the hospital and mentioned Davi going missing. She told me she had reported her concerns, and a DI was investigating."

Graham frowned. "de Silva."

"Yep. At first, she thought he was genuine, but when he told her Davi was stealing drugs and that they were looking for him, she became suspicious."

"Why?"

"Because Davi had seemed scared of de Silva and because he had warned her that staff were coming under pressure to steal drugs."

"Did he tell her where the pressure was coming from?"

"No. After de Silva told her Davi was a thief, she wondered if he was, but she had other reasons to suspect the DI was lying. She had done a stock check after Davi didn't show up for work, and everything was there. The next morning – yesterday, opiates were missing."

"And she realised de Silva had signed in the night before?"

"Exactly. She also told me that a porter – I assume she meant Sim Kumar, the man I spoke to yesterday – had told her that Priya Mendis was covering things up."

Graham stroked his chin. "So, we're on the right track."

"And that's why Priya wanted rid of us. Elize can't be sure Mendis is involved, but I think she suspects her. She's frightened because if Mendis and de Silva are on the take, she has nowhere to turn."

"If she's telling the truth, she's got every reason to be worried. She could be next on their list."

"I believe her. She wanted you to tell Ranil about her suspicions, and I hope you don't mind, but I invited her for a ship tour tomorrow at the same time as Ranil."

"As long as you think we can trust her. Did you tell her anything about our involvement?"

Gwen shook her head. "Too risky. For us and for her because if she knows they killed Davi, she might do a runner, and that would put her in danger. de Silva thinks he's got her convinced for now. You never know, he might leave the pharmacy alone and start on the wards... or even stop altogether for a while."

"That would depend on who's wagging the dog."

"Indeed. Anyway, now you're up to date, shall we head inside?"

Graham nodded. They both stood and scanned the visitors piling into the hospital, waiting for an opportunity to enter unnoticed.

"There," Gwen said, pointing to a group of people getting off a bus just inside the grounds. Gwen tagged onto the back of the crowd, worming her way into the centre. Graham kept away from her but did the same.

Once inside, they peeled away and met in a busy hospital corridor. Certain she hadn't seen Priya Mendis or Rohan de Silva, Gwen relaxed. "This way."

When they reached Ward 17, Graham stopped at the desk to speak to the nurse in charge. "Hello. I'm Dr Graham Bentley from the cruise ship *Coral Queen*. Might we see Mr Benjamin Thompson?"

"Of course. Follow me."

"If the surgeon is satisfied he's well enough, we'd be happy to take him back on board today. His daughter is eager to have him back with the family."

Graham wasn't exactly lying. He told Gwen how he'd spoken to Mrs Thompson-Smith before leaving the ship to meet Gwen, and he'd asked how she'd feel about her father being discharged to the ship's infirmary. She'd been delighted.

"You can ask his deputy. He'll be here soon," the nurse said, smiling. "Here he is. I'll leave you to it."

Ben's eyes lit up on seeing them both. "It's nice to see a friendly face. The guy they've put in the bed next to me doesn't speak English and scowls the whole time. The staff are marvellous, but they're too busy to sit and chat."

"What happened to Sim?" Gwen asked.

"About three hours after you left yesterday, they moved him."

Gwen's stomach felt as though a weight of lead had landed on it.

Ben lowered his voice. "But not before we had a chat. He was keen to tell me how much he'd changed and how sorry he was for getting involved in drugs."

Graham and Gwen sat down, moving chairs closer. "Did he say anything else?" Gwen noticed the man in the next bed snoring. The one on the other side was newly made up, ready for the next inhabitant.

"He said to tell you to be careful, Sister, and not to trust the man who visited him. He told me Detective Inspector de Silva is a dirty cop, but I'm guessing you knew that already?"

"Did he mention anyone else?" Graham asked.

"Not by name, but he said there's a powerful politician with links to the hospital. That's all he would say, except that they were buying off pharmacists and pharmacy technicians to pilfer. If they don't comply, those without family are threatened. I think that was all he knew. He's terrified. I can tell you that much."

"Do you know who arranged for him to be moved?"

"I assumed it was that dodgy detective, but later on I heard a nurse moaning about moving him to a side room on his own. The nurse said he would be lonely and that Doctor Ralik, or something like that, should know better."

"Could it have been Dr Malik?" Graham asked, frowning.

"Might have been. The nurse had a strong accent, and my hearing's not so good these days. The strange thing is that a doctor came to visit Sim shortly before he was moved. He wasn't my surgeon, but he sat down and said he wanted a word with me."

Gwen and Graham exchanged a glance.

"What about?" Gwen asked.

"He asked where I was from and what had happened to me. I told him how you two had diagnosed me, then he asked about you. He said he'd seen you both not long before he came to the ward, and that you…" he looked at Graham, "…and he had trained together."

"Interesting," said Graham. "That sounds like Dr Malik. We ran into him yesterday while I was catching up with an old friend."

"He kept looking around like. It was only after hearing the nurse muttering that I realised it was him getting Sim moved."

"Did he ask you anything specific about us?" Gwen asked.

"Not really. I got the impression he was fishing for information and wanted to say more. I told him nothing." Ben beamed.

Gwen saw anger cloud Graham's eyes for a moment, but he concealed it well when he spoke to Ben. "We're hoping to get you back to the ship today, if you'd like to come?"

"I'd love that," Ben said, grinning.

"You'll need to stay in the infirmary for a few days," Gwen added.

"That would be wonderful. I'm sure I'll be well looked after, and I've never been a fan of spicy food. They do their best here, but most of the relatives bring in their own food supplies for the incumbents, which just about spells it out."

Gwen was pleased to see how perky Ben was, and she would be relieved to have him moved.

"We'll stay for the ward round then and make arrangements with the medical team. Would your daughter be happy to collect you by taxi, or would you like us to arrange something?"

"You've done enough, Dr Bentley, and you, Sister. Our budget can stretch to a taxi. Just get me cleared, and I'll make the call. There's just one thing you can do for me."

"What's that?" Gwen asked.

"Can you check if Sim's all right? He's been through a lot."

"We'll try," she said, "but we don't want to get him into any trouble."

Gwen saw a doctor, followed by a small entourage, enter the ward. She was relieved to divert Ben's attention away from any more questions, just in case he let something slip.

17

"I'm glad we got that sorted," said Graham as they left the hospital, not stopping for food even though he hadn't eaten since the night before. He hadn't told Gwen, but he'd been up for a few hours during the night helping the new doctor with a crew member who had gone into labour eight weeks prematurely. There hadn't been time to summon help, but it turned out their new locum was more than qualified to deliver and incubate a premature baby, having worked in community hospitals.

Thankfully, both mother and daughter were fine after their ordeal and had been transferred to the renowned De Soysa Maternity Hospital.

He heard Gwen's phone ring. "It's Nalini," she said.

Graham took her elbow, propelling her forward. “Let’s get away from here before we become even bigger targets. We’ve been lucky so far, but I don’t want to push it.”

Gwen took the call, walking and talking at the same time. “Thank you, Nalini,” she said, ending the call.

“Are you hungry?” he asked. He wanted to know what the call was about, but he needed to eat.

“Yes. You?” She shot him a sideways glance as if recognising his exhaustion.

He nodded. “How about the Hilton? It’s been a haven for us so far.”

On the walk, Gwen told him the details of the call. “Tiffany has spoken to the detective she mentioned.”

“I’d forgotten about him,” said Graham. “To be honest, I’m wary of involving any of the police.”

“Apparently, this Arjun Nanayakkara will help us. Nalini says Tiffany gave him my number and he’ll be in touch.”

Graham felt a knot in his chest. “She didn’t tell Arjun where she was staying, did she?”

“No. But I’m sure it wouldn’t be hard for him to trace the call.”

“Blast! We don’t even know if we can trust this guy.”

“Tiff’s usually an excellent judge of character.”

Graham exhaled a long breath. That wasn't the point! They couldn't risk going on gut feeling and instinct when so much was at stake.

They were quiet on entering the Hilton's restaurant, both seemingly lost in thoughts and fears about what to do next. The first thing Graham needed to do was eat. "Let's not discuss any of this over lunch. We'll move to a conference room or something afterwards."

"Good plan." Gwen looked as tired as he felt. She, too, had had an unexpected detour the night before. It worried him that she was staying at the YMCA, and even more so now he knew she had gone to meet someone without telling him. He doubted she had slept much, either. A lot had happened to them in a short space of time. What disturbed him more than anything was that his old university pal Imran Malik could be wrapped up in this. He had topped the class for the whole of the first year while the rest of them caught up. All he ever seemed to do was study. Whenever they spoke, it was all about Imran's dreams and expectations. He was always heading to the top, but Graham hadn't considered he might sell his soul to get there. When Gwen had confirmed their suspicions that Priya Mendis was involved, he'd hoped Imran wouldn't be. He rubbed his head.

"Here," Gwen said. "Take these." She handed him a couple of paracetamol, which he took, swallowing them down with a glass of water.

Over lunch, he told her about the newborn and sang the praises of their new team member. Gwen listened. She was a good listener.

Their desserts had just been served when Gwen's phone pinged. She looked at the screen.

"It's from Arjun. He's sent an address and wants us to meet him."

Graham sighed. Could this get any worse? "Where and when?"

"He says it's not safe to meet in Colombo and wants us to meet him at an address on the outskirts. Three o'clock this afternoon."

"At least we've got time for dessert and coffee," said Graham grimly. He hoped this would not be their last meal.

It appeared Gwen was having second thoughts too. "Maybe you should let Jack in on the secret and tell him what we're doing."

"I'll call him straight after this. Now come on, tuck in." Jack Waverley was the ship's chief of security. Graham had considered speaking to him before leaving that morning but had felt it wasn't his call to make. At least if he didn't return to the ship, they could put out a search for him. On that note, he broached the subject that had been on his mind since earlier. "Gwen. How would you feel about sharing a phone tracker with me?"

"I've been wondering the same thing. That way, if we get separated, at least we'll know where the other person is."

"I'm so relieved to hear you say that. I thought you might object."

"I think I've known you long enough to realise you're not a stalker. And these things can be switched off, right?"

"Yes, they can," he said, feeling himself relax as the food helped regulate his blood sugar.

"We've still got time for a quiet meeting before we leave to meet Arjun."

They left the restaurant and found space off the lobby. Graham phoned Jack Waverley while Gwen kept an eye out for anyone looking suspicious. It was a long and difficult conversation, which Jack listened to without interruption and which went better than Graham had expected. When he'd finished, Jack said, "Be careful, Graham. Corruption in these places goes deep, but there are still some good cops. I've got a trustworthy contact. Say the word, and I'll put in a call, or we can do it together."

"That's reassuring, Jack. Thank you."

"If you like, I can give you a wiretap as well."

"That's excellent. Could you leave it at the port entrance, and we'll pick it up on our way to meet this copper? Can you look him up for us? Arjun Nanayakkara."

"Will do."

18

Gwen drove their borrowed car to the address Arjun had texted her, using an app on her phone to navigate. The journey took them into a sprawling industrial estate on the outskirts of Colombo. The building they were heading to was attached to the side of what appeared to be a small warehouse.

As soon as they stepped out of the car, a tall man in his late thirties motioned to them. He had sharp, aquiline features and dark skin. "You must be Gwen, and I'm told you're Graham," he said.

"And you must be Arjun," said Gwen, walking towards him.

"Come inside. It's safe here."

"Thank you for agreeing to meet us, Detective

Nanayakkara," Gwen began, her voice wavering slightly as she fought to maintain her composure and her fear that he might have led them into a trap.

"Please, call me Arjun."

"I'm not sure how much Gwen's cousin has told you," Graham said.

Gwen noticed a light in Arjun's deep brown eyes at the mention of her cousin. Perhaps they were safe after all. All the same, it was reassuring that Graham was wearing a wire and that the security team on board the *Coral Queen* could listen in.

"I've just brewed some coffee. Why don't you tell me the story from your perspective while I pour?"

"Okay," said Gwen, exhaling. "We believe... well, we know... that one of your colleagues, Detective Rohan de Silva, is involved in illegal activities that may pose a serious threat to Tiffany's life. And he murdered a man in cold blood."

Arjun handed her and Graham mugs of strong coffee, frowning. "Help yourselves to milk and sugar," he gestured towards a tray on an otherwise tidy desk.

Gwen poured milk into her drink, but Graham opted for it black. She imagined it was because they had drunk a fair amount of goat's milk since arriving in Sri Lanka, which was sweeter than either of them was used to.

Arjun's brow furrowed, and after taking a sip of

his own milky coffee, which she watched him add three sugars to, he said, "Tiffany mentioned her pharmacy friend's death. No body matching his description has been reported, so I haven't made inquiries other than gathering a little background in secret. He has been reported as missing by a manager at the National Hospital and is suspected of drug dealing. I didn't realise the man's death involved a police officer."

Gwen and Graham took turns recounting what they had gleaned so far without mentioning Priya Mendis or Imran Malik. "Tiffany was in her condo when de Silva shot Davi Ranasinghe. Another man was with him, but we don't know whether he was a police officer. Tiffany believes they shot Davi in front of her to warn her that when they want her to do something, she has to obey."

"That must have been an awful shock for her. She didn't go into detail when I spoke to her. It's brazen to kill a man in her home, desperate almost."

"The men left the body in her condo and insisted she was not to go to the police. They said they would be back and that if she didn't do what they asked, she'd get the same treatment. She believes her friend refused to steal drugs from the hospital and had planned to run away," Gwen said.

"How can you be sure the dead man is innocent?"

"Through various sources, people who knew him can't believe he would be involved in anything like that. And there's a witness who was involved in the racket until recently who confirms de Silva is crooked," said Graham.

"By involved in the racket, you mean, a drug addict and a thief?" Arjun sounded sceptical.

"He's clean now," said Gwen, folding her arms.

"And this man's name is?"

"I'm not prepared to name him. But believe me, we have spoken to other people who have corroborated that Davi was not a drug thief, and one who suspects de Silva's involvement," said Gwen.

"I understand you are finding it difficult to trust anyone, but unless you trust me, it's going to be impossible for me to help you."

"We're concerned for the man's safety. A doctor had him moved to a room on his own in the hospital, and we don't want anything to happen to him. Plus, the other people have spoken in confidence," said Graham. "Tiffany is at risk until this matter is resolved, but please don't take our hesitation personally."

"Okay," Arjun said, scribbling notes in a small leather-bound notebook he produced from his pocket. "Other than the shooting, your witness, and, erm, other sources, do you have any solid evidence to support that the homicide is related to DI de Silva's involvement a drug racket?"

"Nothing concrete," Gwen admitted, her voice heavy with frustration. "I visited a patient from the cruise ship yesterday, and Detective de Silva visited the witness while I was there. de Silva later turned up at a restaurant where Graham and I were dining. He must have traced us. He's also been asking people about us."

"He spoke to the ward nurse before I left our patient, and at the restaurant quizzed me about my visit. He had also been told we took a tour of the hospital and its pharmacy and was checking our story about being medics from the *Coral Queen*. For now, we believe he's convinced we know nothing about him or the crime he committed."

"That's good. Although the de Silva I know is a cautious man who keeps a tight team around him."

"You already have your suspicions, don't you?" Graham said.

"From time to time, there have been rumours about him, but no proof. I have what you would call a snitch who has made similar accusations, but nothing with evidence that will bring him down." Arjun's eyes narrowed as he finished his coffee. "This is serious, and I'm inclined to believe you, but you realise I have to be careful. I'll see what I can find out," he promised, closing his notebook with a decisive snap. "In the meantime, I suggest you both steer clear of de Silva and avoid drawing any undue attention to yourselves."

"Our thoughts exactly," Gwen agreed, feeling a small flicker of hope ignite within her chest. "We just want to protect Tiffany. If de Silva finds out where she is..."

"Understood. They won't hear it from me, but you should warn her not to phone again. Make sure it's you who contacts her, and use a landline." Arjun offered them a reassuring smile, extending his hand to shake theirs in turn. "We should meet again tomorrow, and I'll give you an update. It's best for us to communicate face-to-face. Here is best."

"What is this place?" Graham asked.

"You probably gathered, it's an industrial estate. The warehouses used to store fishing equipment and supplies, but now they're mostly empty. I rent this office to meet informers, and collate evidence away from prying eyes."

Gwen thought it was an ideal location to investigate corruption, as long as Arjun was clean.

"Meet me here tomorrow at 8pm."

"I'm afraid we have a dinner date tomorrow. Could we meet the day after?" Gwen suggested.

"Can you make it after your dinner date? I'll aim to be here by 10pm and will wait for you."

Gwen checked with Graham, who nodded. "We'll get here when we can."

"In the meantime, enjoy Sri Lanka and stay away from the hospital. Don't underestimate de Silva. He might have believed your story, but with Tiffany being out of contact, he'll be nervous and therefore more diligent."

"No worries there for now," said Gwen. "She's on leave, and her phone is in Mumbai."

"Clever. Still, be careful where you go, what you say, and who you say it to."

With that, the meeting drew to a close. Gwen and Graham returned to the car for the journey back to the city. Graham drove this time, and Gwen noticed him checking the mirrors all the way.

"We're not being followed," she said.

"What did you make of him?"

"He's got a crush on Tiffany. I'd say that bodes in our favour."

"What makes you think that?"

"Every time we mentioned her, his pupils dilated, and he fiddled with his tie."

Graham shook his head. "We men are so easy to read. Is that what you're saying?"

"Some of you are," Gwen said. *I wish I could read you better,* she thought.

"Are we going to take Arjun's advice and be tourists?"

Gwen prodded his chest where the wire was concealed. Graham nodded. "That's all for now, Jack. Speak later." He switched the microphone off.

Gwen had been debating what to do next in her head. "Part of me wants to say yes, let's be tourists, but I can't relax until we get to the bottom of this. Arjun will have to tread carefully and skirt around his day job. I agree we should stay away from the hospital, and now Ben has been discharged we don't need to go there, but what about checking out our local politician, Priya Mendis?"

"How would we do that?"

"We could find out where her office is and look inside, preferably after dark."

Gwen expected Graham to object and almost hoped he would, but he didn't. He was silent.

19

Graham had returned to the ship to meet with Jack Waverley to discuss their next steps and check on Ben Thompson in the infirmary. Gwen was aware he also had a few medical issues to address. They had agreed to meet at the Hilton once he was finished.

When she caught sight of Graham's tall and handsome frame, Gwen's heart skipped a beat. She told herself it was because of the daring adventure ahead of them, but felt her cheeks burn as he approached.

"Everything okay?"

"Sure."

"Shall we eat first?" Graham's dark brown eyes seemed to look into her soul.

"Why not? We need all the strength we can get. One condition: this time I'm buying."

Graham opened his mouth as if to protest but closed it again. "Agreed."

Over dinner, Graham updated her on the case he'd been called to see. "One of our engineers might have chicken pox. Apparently, he went ashore to meet his family and his kids have all come down with it. He'd not had it as a child. We've isolated him for now so that the rest of the crew who haven't been exposed to chicken pox before, are protected."

"Oh dear."

"The new guy was worried about Mpox, but it looks nothing like it."

"Oh?" Gwen wondered if perhaps their new locum wasn't as proficient as expected.

"Janet assures me he's better at obstetrics and accidents than he is at simple rashes. He was a great help with the premature baby last night."

Gwen hoped the locum wasn't causing Janet too many problems. "I'm sure Bernard will whip him into shape."

"He's on it," Graham said, laughing. "We need to get this business sorted. Mr Thompson told me he hadn't seen de Silva again, but he managed to visit Sim before being discharged. I'd wondered why Imran, a vascular surgeon had visited Sim, but Ben said Sim told him he had a borderline aortic aneurysm requiring ongoing monitoring."

"It's reassuring Imran's visit was genuine," said Gwen thoughtfully.

"There's nothing else new on the Sim front, but he looked to Mr Thompson like he was improving and had received no further visits from de Silva."

"That's a relief. Let's hope the detective continues to leave him alone." Gwen recognised the worry in Graham's eyes. Although the ship was only at half capacity with passengers enjoying their Sri Lankan layover, the crew still had to be cared for. She missed being with them. "Hopefully Arjun will get somewhere. How was Ben himself?"

"Glad to be back on the ship, and especially happy with the food. Brigitte's looking after him. Jack agrees with our view that Arjun is one of the good cops. He's checked him out, and the man has a reputation for honesty and incorruptibility. With Jack's help, I got an address for Mrs Mendis, although I didn't tell him what we were doing tonight. He wouldn't approve." Graham patted his jacket pocket.

They didn't linger after dinner, although part of Gwen would have liked to. Instead, she paid the bill, and after checking around to ensure they weren't being watched, they left the hotel.

Graham entered the address into his phone and

they opted to walk. That way, no taxi driver could inform de Silva where they had been if asked. Gwen believed de Silva had forgotten about them for now, and she would like to keep it that way.

The Colombo sun had set over the bustling streets while they were eating. Now, it was manmade light casting an orange haze around the throngs of people out for the evening. As on the previous evening, the city was as busy as it had been during the day. Fresh aromas of spices and street food mingled with the ever-present diesel fumes, assaulting Gwen's senses. The mixture created a sensory overload that Gwen found both exhilarating and disconcerting.

"Have you ever visited Tiffany here before?" Graham asked.

Gwen knew he was trying to put them both at ease by chatting as they followed the map on his phone. "No. The last few times we've docked here, I've been on duty," Gwen replied. "I was in Colombo for an international nursing conference once, but I didn't get to see much of the city. This is a novel experience, and one I wouldn't want to repeat."

Graham chuckled. "You can say that again! My first encounter with the island was during my time working for Doctors Without Borders. We were stationed in a remote village several hours from here."

Their conversation flowed as they navigated the teeming pavements. Gwen wished they had more time to talk because each story provided another brick in the bridge of understanding that was slowly forming between them. They were moving beyond friendship. But was that what she wanted?

"Watch out!" Graham warned suddenly, grabbing her arm and pulling her back just in time to avoid a speeding tuk-tuk.

"Thanks," she stammered, trying to ignore the warmth radiating from his touch while feeling annoyed with herself for being distracted from the task at hand. She reminded herself firmly: *now is not the time for preoccupation.*

"Here we are," Graham whispered as he stopped short of a modern office building. They waited in the shadow of a nearby shop. Moments later, they watched Priya Mendis's authoritative figure emerge from the entrance, speaking the whole time on her phone. She climbed into a chauffeured limousine without even nodding to the driver. After the driver closed the door, the dark, tinted windows obscured any view of her. The limo moved into traffic and drove away.

"How does she get away with wearing a bright white coat in a dusty city like this?" Gwen asked.

Graham chuckled. "I doubt she spends much time away from her shiny domain."

It was good to see that the building remained well-lit.

"These people work late. Perhaps we should make a move," Gwen said, taking a deep breath before crossing the road. Graham stayed close while scanning the vicinity.

Once they were outside the expansive municipal building, Gwen stopped. They observed the receptionist, who was busy fielding telephone calls. With the practiced ease of those accustomed to moving through a crowd unnoticed, they walked inside confidently. When they arrived at the lifts, they scanned the list of names and floors. Priya Mendis's office was on the second floor.

"Ready?" asked Graham.

"Ready," she replied. The lift was empty when they pressed the button for the second floor. No-one was waiting when they exited into a quiet corridor. Motion sensor lights switched on as they moved unchallenged towards the official's office. The door creaked open with a soft groan as Gwen pushed it open. "Phew. I thought it might be locked."

"Probably leaving it open for the cleaners," said Graham.

Priya Mendis's office was sizeable, with an ornate desk backing onto a window. Gwen peered outside. The view looked out at the rear of the building. Her heart stopped when she saw the cars in the opposite building's car park. "Blimey! It backs onto the police station," she said, quickly closing the blinds.

"We should get on then," said Graham.

Mendis's office was neat, just like the woman herself. Her papers were stacked in an orderly pile on the desk. Expensive-looking paintings hung meticulously on the walls. Gwen fingered a photo of Mendis with an older man and two children aged around six and eight.

Graham was checking through a filing cabinet. "We need to find something – anything – that might incriminate her. The only thing is, I don't know what I'm looking for."

Gwen nodded, her heart pounding as she rifled through the stacks of documents and file folders. "Me neither, but maybe it will be obvious if we find something." Her fingers brushed against a nondescript manila folder tucked away in the top drawer. She pulled it free.

"Found something?" Graham asked, glancing over at her.

"Maybe," Gwen replied, trying to keep her voice steady. "There are lots of legal documents and photographs in here. We should take pictures of everything and get out of here before someone notices. We can look at it later."

"Good idea," he said, pulling out his phone to photograph the contents of the file while she turned the pages.

After finding little else, Gwen's stomach felt increasingly unsettled. It was frustrating. They had found the folder filled with documents and photographs, but without scrutiny, she had no idea whether it was important.

"I'll check the other drawers," Graham whispered, his voice barely audible above the hum of the air-conditioning.

"Right," she murmured. "I wonder if there's a safe."

"Good thought," said Graham, moving away from the desk and checking behind the artwork on the walls. "Here," he said.

"All we need now is the combination," said Gwen, urgently searching through the drawers again.

"She won't have written it down," said Graham.

"No, but she might have the kids' birthdays in her diary," she said, holding up the desk diary and flicking through. She eventually found what she was looking for, and after trying several combinations of the numbers, the safe clicked open.

Graham rummaged inside. "There's a stack of cash in here. This is where she keeps her dirty money."

"Someone's coming!" Gwen moved to the door just as Graham put something in his pocket, closed the safe, and replaced the picture.

The footsteps in the hallway grew louder. Panic surged through Gwen's chest as she realised they were about to be caught. She held her breath.

"Quick!" she hissed, opening the office door and coming face to face with a large woman wearing a sky-blue sari.

The woman jumped before looking angry. She spoke harshly in Sinhalese.

"Sorry, we don't speak Sinhalese," said Gwen.

"I said, who are you and what are you doing in here?" The woman's English was good, which was unfortunate.

"We were hoping to catch Priya," said Gwen.

"You know Mrs Mendis?"

"We met yesterday, and she suggested we stop by to discuss how we can help with the erm... hospital," said Graham, catching on.

"Ah, I see. She didn't mention anything to me, but she has a lot of meetings I'm not aware of. Anyway, you won't find her here again today. She left a while ago for an evening function. I'm Farsal, her secretary. Would you like me to make an appointment for another day?"

"No need," said Gwen. "I've got her number. I'll call her." Gwen wriggled her way past Farsal, whose eyes were narrowing suspiciously.

"Thank you for your help," Graham added, before joining Gwen in a hasty retreat down the corridor. Gwen heard muttering in Sinhalese, and she couldn't determine whether it was aimed at them or at her boss for not keeping her informed.

"That was close," said Graham when they were back out on the street.

"Too close. Thank heavens she didn't insist on taking our names because I'm really not that good at improvisation."

Graham grinned. "I don't know. I thought you were terrific."

Gwen was glad it was dark and he couldn't see her blushing. "What did you take from the safe?"

"This," he said, pulling a USB stick out of his pocket.

"Good work," Gwen said, feeling they were finally getting somewhere.

"I'll take it back to the ship and give it to Jack. It'll be safer trying to find out what's on it from there."

Gwen wished she could go with him, but there were still only a handful of people aware of what they were up to. She didn't want to get anyone else into trouble or put them in a position where they would have to lie for her.

"Call me when you get it open."

"Let me walk you back to the YMCA," said Graham.

"Best not," she replied, her voice unusually thick. "It's not far."

"We'll save the Sky Lounge for another night, then?" There was a seriousness on his face that Gwen found difficult to interpret. A streetlight reflected on his grey sideburns, disappearing into his fair hair.

"I guess so. When I get back to the hostel, I'll call Jack and request a pass for Elize to be sent to my phone. Then I'll ring her to confirm where to meet tomorrow. She might have more information or know if anything else has happened. I'm hoping she'll have news on Davi. They must have moved the body by now."

"Good call. We'll speak soon then."

"Yep." Gwen crossed the road, hurrying back to the YMCA, her mind racing with confusion over her growing feelings for Graham, along with questions about what could be on that memory stick.

20

After a frustrating morning waiting for Graham to contact her, Gwen was about to break her rule and return to the ship when he phoned.

"Sorry I didn't get to call earlier. I've been inundated all morning. We had a few sick people, and I've been summoned to virtual corporate meetings with the cruise line this afternoon. You would have been too if you were here. They want to take the opportunity of the delayed departure and our half-empty ship to introduce plans for the future."

Gwen hated missing out on important developments, but Graham was an excellent communicator and would pass on any necessary information. "I understand. That makes sense. Have you had time to find out what's on that memory stick?"

"Jack left it with the IT department and asked them to check it first thing. Unfortunately, they haven't been able to get past the encryption. I didn't want to draw any further attention to it, so it's back with me. Did you get anything from Elize?"

"Yes, she said the police had found a body in the river and concluded it was a mugging or drug deal gone wrong. She doesn't know for certain whether it's Davi."

She heard Graham sigh. "It will be, though. At least Tiffany's off the hook for the murder."

"Unless they decide she was the dealer," said Gwen. "Who knows what de Silva will do next? Or Priya Mendis, for that matter?"

"She's not that approachable. We can hope her secretary didn't mention our visit to her office. I also doubt Mrs Mendis is the most forgiving of bosses, so the less said, the better."

Gwen felt better about that. "Good point. Mendis would most likely blame her secretary for our intrusion, so we might have got away with that one."

"Right. I'd better go now. See you at five-thirty for the guided tours."

"Great. I told Elize I'd meet her outside and bring her in."

"Okay. See you later."

Gwen ended the call, not knowing what to do with the rest of her afternoon. Maybe a sleep wouldn't go amiss.

People laughing in the corridor outside her room roused Gwen from a deep sleep. She groaned until she looked at the time and then leapt out of bed. If she didn't get a move on, she would be late for her meeting with Elize. After a quick shower, she slipped into a summer dress that would suffice for later. She didn't want to be caught out again if the restaurant Ranil took them to was on the posh side. This outfit would work if there was no time to get to her stateroom to change into something better. She shoved jeans and a summer jumper into a bag to change into after dinner before driving to meet Arjun.

Gwen collected the car from the car park and drove to the port. Elize was waiting at the gate, so she motioned for her to get in. After showing her pass and Elize's guest pass to the security guard, she drove right up to the ship and parked in the space reserved for tourist buses, taxis, and minivans.

"Here we are," said Gwen.

Elize's eyes widened. "I've never been this close to one of these cruise liners. It's massive."

"We call it a small village because that's how many people are on board at any one time. Come on. I expect Graham and Ranil will be waiting for us."

Gwen took Elize further along the dockside to the crew entrance. Ravanos, one of the ship's security guards, was checking passes. "Hello Gwen. Dr Bentley told me to expect you and a guest."

Gwen handed over her ID card for swiping and showed her phone, which contained Elize's pass, then placed her belongings in a tray for the security conveyor belt. She turned to Elize. "You'll need to put your bag and phone into a tray."

"Right." Elize followed suit.

"They go through scanners, like at airports," she explained.

Gwen then walked through the metal detector while the other security guard beckoned for Elize to do the same.

Once through security, they found Graham and Ranil in earnest conversation.

"Hello again," said Graham to Elize.

"Hi," she replied. "Sorry to gatecrash your tour, but Gwen offered." Elize was looking at Ranil.

"No problem, Elize. It's good to see you outside of

work. We rarely get the opportunity to chat informally."

Gwen wondered if Graham had shared Elize's concerns with the consultant but doubted he would have done so here, with the crew passing back and forth to get on and off the ship.

"Welcome to our domain," said Graham. "Where would you like to start?"

Ranil gave them all a wide smile. "I'd like to see everything, as long as we have time to explore the medical centre, please."

"We'll save that until last, as we're near the engines and the primary hub of the crew area. Let's start there." Graham's eyes shone. Gwen could see he was just as excited as she was about showing their guests around the *Coral Queen*.

"It will be a whistle-stop tour," she added. "It takes weeks to get to know where everything is, and then some."

"Then please lead the way," said Ranil. "I've booked a dinner table for eight."

"Right. Let's go."

Graham led them through the maze of narrow corridors. They descended several flights of steep stairs, the temperature rising noticeably. Gwen noticed Elize gripping the handrail tightly. "It takes a while to get your sea legs," she said sympathetically. "Even when we're docked, the ship moves slightly."

The distant thrumming of engines grew louder as they reached the engineering deck. The corridors here were lined with pipes and technical equipment, all carefully labelled.

"This is the heart of the ship," Graham announced as they entered the engine control room. Banks of monitors displayed various readings: temperature, pressure, fuel consumption. Several engineers in blue overalls looked up from their stations, nodding in greeting. Officers wore white uniforms with gold stripes on their epaulettes, signalling their seniority.

"That's our chief systems engineer, Aryna Petrova," Graham called out to a distinguished-looking woman with long hair tied in a tight bun. "Do you mind if we show our guests around?"

"Not at all." The engineer smiled warmly, her accent American, though Gwen was aware Aryna was Russian born. Her voice was smooth and mellow. "We're currently running on shore power, but I can show you our key systems."

Aryna led them to a large display screen. "These are our main diesel engines. Together, they generate 62,400 kilowatts – enough to power a small city."

Ranil studied the display with interest. "The environmental controls must be impressive."

"They are," Aryna agreed. "We have state-of-the-art emission control systems and water treatment plants. Nothing goes overboard that shouldn't."

They moved through the engineering spaces, passing the massive shaft alley where the propeller systems connected. The heat was intense.

"The crew areas are essentially a ship within a ship," Graham explained, shouting above the noise as he walked quickly. "Our engineers are the finest in the fleet, but I would say that, wouldn't I? They are waiting for parts to arrive from India before we can leave port."

Pleased to escape the noise of the engine rooms, they climbed the stairs again. Gwen gestured to a recreational room where off-duty crew members were playing table tennis and watching TV. "We have rank-tiered dining rooms, a gym, and recreation areas. It helps create a home away from home," she said.

"How many crew members are there?" Elize asked, peering through the doorway.

"Usually around two thousand," Gwen replied. "Though we're currently running with reduced numbers. Some have taken the opportunity to go ashore while they can."

"Next stop, the bridge," Graham announced. "It's quite a contrast to where we've just been."

They took a lift, which whisked them up to deck twelve where Rosemary Inglis, a security officer, waited to escort them. Visitors were always accompanied by security when entering the bridge or security areas. Stepping onto the bridge, they entered another world – all gleaming technology and panoramic windows. Captain Peter Jenson, a tall man with short greying hair, greeted them warmly.

"I heard we were having guests today. Welcome," he said with a smile. "Please feel free to look around. My first officer will explain things."

"This is incredible." Ranil's eyes shone as he took in the sophisticated navigation equipment. "How do you coordinate everything?"

The first officer, Nicholas Evans, pointed to various stations. "Navigation, communications, safety systems – each has dedicated officers. We constantly monitor the weather, other vessels, and all ship systems."

Gwen watched as Elize examined the radar displays. "The technology is amazing," she said. "It's so different from hospital systems."

"Different purpose, same principle," Graham replied. "Everything monitored, everything logged."

"The ship runs an autopilot system when we're out at sea," Nicholas explained.

After spending fifteen minutes exploring the bridge, Rosemary cleared her throat, signalling that they should move on.

Proceeding to the passenger areas, they entered the main atrium. A crystal chandelier cascaded down through three decks, and glass lifts glided silently up and down. Classical music played softly in the background.

"Most passengers enter through here," Gwen explained. "First impressions count."

They walked through the ship's heart, passing high-end boutiques and art and photo galleries.

"We have a main restaurant that spans two floors," Graham said, "plus five speciality venues and a twenty-four-hour buffet. The main dining room is through here..."

They peered into the two-storey space, where staff were serving dinner to the guests already seated. The hum of conversation, punctuated by laughter, reached their ears. As soon as passengers left, the waiters cleared and set the tables, ready for the next guests to enter. Crystal glasses gleamed on white tablecloths.

"The logistics must be overwhelming," Elize commented.

"It's like running a small village," Gwen agreed. "Everything has to be planned meticulously. Food, water, fuel, medical supplies..."

They walked the length of the ship to the theatre, its plush red seats beginning to fill for the first show of the evening.

The pool deck was next, two outdoor swimming pools glinting in the early evening sun. "This area is packed on sea days," Gwen explained. "Though I prefer the crew pool when it's open – much quieter! There's also an indoor pool."

Finally, they took the lifts back down to deck two, where the medical centre was located. Graham swiped his card, and they entered the state-of-the-art facility. "And this is where our magic happens."

As they followed Graham, Ranil and Elize examined everything. "This is impressive," Ranil said, inspecting the diagnostic equipment. "You have an X-ray, as well as ultrasound and lab facilities..."

"We do, and there's an infirmary and an intensive care bed. We have to be prepared for anything," Gwen said, showing them the infirmary. "Heart attacks, broken bones, appendicitis – we can't just call an ambulance when we're miles out."

Elize was paying particular attention to the medication storage area. The pharmacist studied the keypad entry system and security cameras with professional interest.

"Your security systems are impressive," Elize said, examining the electronic logging system.

"They have to be," Graham responded, exchanging a meaningful look with Gwen. "We can't afford any... irregularities. Every tablet is accounted for."

"And paid for," Gwen chuckled.

They showed them the small ward and the consultation rooms. Gwen noted that Ben Thompson was no longer there. "We can stabilise most conditions," Graham explained. "Though serious cases get evacuated when possible. One of our passengers had his appendix out a few days ago."

Gwen wanted to ask when he had been discharged, but that would reveal she wasn't currently working onboard. "We usually hold two surgeries a day, but we've cut it down to just one in the morning while we're in port. A nurse or medic – sometimes both – are always on call."

Ranil checked his watch. "This has been fascinating, and I'd love to stay longer, but we should head to dinner soon. Thank you both for the tour."

As they prepared to leave, Gwen caught Elize contemplating the medication security system one last time. Perhaps seeing how things could be done properly would help her address the issues at the National Hospital.

"Shall we get changed and meet you at the restaurant?" Graham asked Ranil.

"Perfect. I'll text you the address," Ranil replied. "Would you like to join us, Elize?"

"I'd love to," she said. Gwen escorted Ranil and Elize through security and watched them go. Perhaps Elize would share her concerns with the friendly consultant. Gwen hoped their evening would bring more insights into the troubling situation at the hospital.

21

Gwen parked the car closer to the building where they were meeting Arjun than Graham had the day before. It ended up concealed in the dark, behind a row of overgrown shrubbery near the disused warehouse. She removed the keys from the ignition and was about to open the door when Graham put a hand on her arm.

"Wait a minute."

"What's the matter?" Gwen asked.

"I don't know, but I can't see Arjun."

"He's probably inside the office where we met yesterday."

"Maybe, but let's be cautious. He hasn't answered the text telling him we're on our way."

They were both tired. Dinner had gone on longer

than they had imagined. Any other time, it would have been a joy to be eating authentic Sri Lankan cuisine in pleasant company. The conversations had briefly touched on the problems at the hospital, and Ranil had reassured Graham that his other old friend Imran Malik was not involved in anything illegal. "He's ambitious but still devout, Graham."

"So why did he visit our patient on Ward 17 and ask questions about us?" Gwen had asked.

"He wanted to apologise for being dismissive when you met. He came to me later and asked me to do it for him. I forgot."

Elize had concurred with Ranil, stating that Dr Malik was legitimate and, if anything, was as concerned about drug dealing as she was. Graham had asked why he had the ex-porter Sim moved if he was innocent.

"Because Priya Mendis asked him to. She told Imran the man had stolen from the hospital and should be kept isolated so that he couldn't access drugs on the ward."

Graham had seemed relieved and gave the impression he wanted to discuss the drug dealing matter in more detail, but Ranil had been quick to change the topic. Gwen couldn't blame him for wanting to enjoy a night out. She hadn't been able to gauge whether Elize had shared her concerns with Ranil in any detail prior to dinner, but they seemed at ease with each other. As Gwen and Graham had agreed not to share what they knew, it would have been pointless to press the matter.

Graham opened the door quietly, with Gwen following suit. They closed the car doors with a gentle push after climbing out. All was silent apart from aeroplanes flying overhead at regular intervals.

"We must be under a flight path," said Gwen.

Graham didn't reply. The air was thick with tension, like the quiet before a storm. He was making her nervous. Gwen's hands shook as she locked the old BMW. Graham remained still, studying their surroundings.

"Follow me," he said.

Gwen stayed close to his heels as they tiptoed around a tall palm tree, moving stealthily towards the office. Peering through the window, what she saw caused her jaw to drop. A chair had been toppled over and the contents of the desk lay scattered on the floor.

With her pulse threatening to burst through her eardrums, she whispered, "Now what?"

Graham put his fingers to his lips, turned the door handle, and nudged it open. With no-one in sight, they both stepped inside. Arjun's coat was hanging on the back of the door. "He's here somewhere. We need to find him."

Every instinct told Gwen they should run, but they were stuck. They couldn't call the police, and they couldn't leave Arjun to his fate when it was they who'd got him into whatever had caused this mess. The light in the office was still on. She tiptoed over to the kettle. "It's still warm."

Graham was staring at the contents on the floor, frowning.

They went outside, and Gwen peeped around the side of the building. "His car's here, which is good, but there's also a van, which is not so good."

Graham peeked around her shoulder. "They must be inside the warehouse. Let's go."

She nodded solemnly. "Are you sure we should do this?"

A spark of determination flickered in Graham's eyes. "Whatever happened in that office wasn't friendly. We can't leave him. These people are desperate."

"Okay." Every footstep, though quiet, sounded loud to Gwen's ears in her heightened state of alertness. Discarded cigarette butts lay scattered outside the warehouse entrance; one was still smouldering. Gwen's heart pounded in her chest. She wondered if Graham felt the same tension.

"Two of them at least," said Gwen, pointing to the butts.

"Okay," said Graham, grabbing a large piece of wood lying on the floor. "We find Arjun and get out as fast as possible."

Gwen wasn't sure Graham would be able to use his weapon, but if it made him feel better, who was she to argue? "If only we could call the police," she whispered.

"We can't. Stay close, Gwen. We don't know what we're walking into," Graham warned, his hand reaching for hers. Their fingers intertwined. Gwen felt a rush of heat as his grip tightened, urging her to move forward.

As they inched inside the warehouse, she felt her heart would explode. But with every step, and with Graham next to her, she grew stronger.

About six feet inside, they paused, listening. All was quiet. Graham released her hand.

"Let's split up," he suggested. His eyes were on the rickety staircase that led to an upper level. "You check down here while I look upstairs. We'll cover more ground that way."

She wanted to refuse but was as keen as he was to get this over with and escape this place. "What do we do if we find these people?" Gwen asked, concern furrowing her brow.

"Keep our phones on vibrate. Text one another if we see anything. Don't do anything rash; nothing about this place is safe, Gwen." He gave her hand a reassuring squeeze, but it trembled just like hers. "Just be careful, and yell or scream if you're in trouble."

"Promise you'll do the same," she insisted, her eyes locking onto his. "Maybe not the screaming part," she added, forcing a smile. There was so much left unsaid between them, but now wasn't the time for confessions or declarations. They had a job to do, and Arjun's life might be hanging in the balance. If he was still alive.

"I promise," Graham assured her.

They separated, each moving cautiously. Gwen watched Graham climb the creaky stairs, wincing with every step he took.

Once he was out of sight, she navigated her way through the maze of crates, trying not to step on the debris on the ground floor. Her eyes strained to see in the dim light, but she didn't dare use the torch on her phone. The air was thick with the scent of decay, and the fishy odour confirmed what Arjun had told them about its prior use. She pushed forward, refusing to be deterred. Suddenly, she heard voices. A man was coming down the stairs. Gwen hid behind a steel support, hoping Graham was doing the same.

22

Graham was relieved to leave the wooden stairs that seemed determined to betray him. He stepped cautiously onto the upper level, scanning the shadows for any signs of Arjun. Even the floorboards here groaned beneath his weight, quieter than the stairs, nevertheless, a haunting reminder of the danger present. After searching for what felt like an eternity, he stopped breathing. A shuffling noise caught his attention, prompting him to jump behind a stack of empty crates. He held his breath as someone passed, heading for the stairs.

"I'll see if I can get a signal outside," the man called to someone behind him.

Graham waited until the man descended the stairs, creating a racket. Reassured that Gwen would have heard him, Graham stayed put. He debated whether to confront the guy, but knew he was not a fighter, and knowing another person was up here, it would be suicide.

Once he was certain the man was outside, Graham exhaled. Screwing up his nose to escape the stench of fish, he waited a moment and checked his phone. Gwen hadn't texted, which was unsurprising given the lack of signal. Hearing no further noise, he assumed she was all right. Leaving the lump of wood behind, he took cautious steps in the direction the man had come from, stopping dead when he heard a gruff voice in the distance talking to someone. *Please God, not three of them.*

Graham pressed forward until he realised he had gone too far. A huge, wild-eyed figure lurched towards him, brandishing a knife that glinted in the darkness.

"Put that away!" said Graham, sounding far more authoritative than he felt. He had learned during his years in accident and emergency, and even on board the cruise ship, how to dodge dangerous assailants, usually patients.

The crazed man hesitated, snarling at Graham. "Who are you?"

"Rohan sent me to check on you. Have you got him?"

"Yeah, he's back there." The man inclined his head. "We couldn't get anything out of him. Don't worry, we followed instructions. He's alive... for now. Does he want us to finish him?"

"No. He's on his way. I'll stand guard. He said you two could leave."

"Are you sure? Marli's just gone to call him."

"There's no signal, which is why Rohan couldn't let you know I was on my way. You go."

The man didn't seem unhappy about leaving. "Right. Tell Rohan we moved the body as instructed last night."

"He already knows," said Graham.

Graham struggled to breathe after the second man left. He hoped the first hadn't caught de Silva and that he was just as gullible as the beast he'd just encountered.

Relieved to hear the van screeching away in the darkness, Graham saw Gwen.

"They've gone," she said.

"Yes, I made a judgement call which turned out to be right. I told the giant who was about to attack me with a knife that de Silva had sent me. We need to hurry in case either of them makes a phone call."

"Clever move. I'm impressed, and amazed they believed you."

"He wasn't the brightest tool in the box, but no-one was more pleased he believed my story than me. Otherwise, he might have used his weapon."

"Speaking of weapons, where's yours?"

Graham felt embarrassed. "I left it behind some crates, it's not like I would have used it. Anyway, it's also fortunate neither of us got into trouble, as there's no phone signal."

Gwen looked at her phone. "You're right. Have you found Arjun?"

"No but I think he's up here. The all-in wrestler told me someone's back there." He pointed to the back of the warehouse. "Let's not waste any more time."

As they moved, Graham admired Gwen's bravery. Despite her own fears and the dangers they faced, she had put herself in harm's way, just as he had. That was a near miss, as the adrenaline surging through his body reminded him. He hoped that when this was all over, he and Gwen would have the chance to explore what their newfound bond meant. But for now, they had a mission to complete.

"Arjun!" called Graham, his voice echoing through the cavernous space. "Can you hear me?"

"Over there." Gwen pointed towards a narrow gap, barely visible in the gloom.

They headed towards the passage and followed a winding corridor, opening each door as they went.

The air grew colder as they ventured further inside, their breaths turning to mist in the darkness.

"Arjun!" Gwen called.

As they rounded a corner, Graham heard a faint rustling sound. They exchanged a glance, hope springing up in their eyes. The rustling grew louder as they approached a dimly lit door at the end of the corridor. Gwen reached for the handle and slowly pushed it open, revealing a small room.

"Arjun!" Graham said, relief washing over him as he caught sight of the detective huddled in the corner. He was bound tightly to a wooden chair and gagged. His bruised and bloodied face testified to the beating he'd suffered.

"Thank God," Gwen said, heading towards him and untying the gag from his mouth.

"I thought I was done for," he said. "I was praying they didn't get you as well."

"Let's get you out of here," Graham said urgently, stepping forward to untie the knots in the rope holding Arjun captive. "I sold one of them a story, but it won't take long for them to realise I'm not working with Rohan."

Rubbing a swollen lip, Arjun said, "de Silva figured out what I was doing after I made discreet inquiries. He sent his goons after me to find out how much I know. He must have had a tracker put in my car because I was certain I wasn't being followed."

As they helped Arjun to his feet, Graham's thoughts raced, trying to work out their next steps. One thing was certain: this situation was becoming too dangerous for all of them.

They went outside and found Arjun's car was still there. He checked it over before removing a device from inside the boot, giving a solemn nod. "I'll leave this here," he said, climbing inside. "I assume you brought your car?"

"Yes," said Graham.

"Then follow me."

"Where are we going?" Graham asked.

"To see someone before Gwen's cousin is framed for murder." Arjun's dark eyes settled on Gwen.

"But we heard that a body was fished out of the river. The police told one of our sources it was a drug deal gone wrong," Gwen said grimly.

"The goon I met said it was him and his mate who moved the body," said Graham. "Shame I left our security chief's wire on board the *Coral Queen*."

"That may be, but de Silva's got it set up so that when the time comes, there'll be no way she can prove her innocence."

Graham felt a chill run down his spine, his stomach twisting in knots as he looked at Gwen's pale complexion under the moonlight. de Silva must be getting desperate, and it wouldn't be long before he discovered that Gwen and Tiffany were related. After that, who knew what he would do?

"Do you think he found out about the memory stick?" Gwen asked.

"What memory stick?" Arjun asked.

Graham reached inside his trouser pocket and raised it in the air. "We paid Priya Mendis's office a visit last night, but this is encrypted."

Arjun's eyes filled with hope. "Where was it?"

"In her safe," said Gwen.

Grinning for the first time since they had found him, Arjun opened his driver's door. "Keep hold of it. Let's go before they come back. With what you've got there, we might have the evidence we need to expose de Silva and Priya Mendis in one go."

"Let's get going." Gwen was already heading to where she'd parked the car when they arrived.

23

Arjun pulled up outside a small police station on the outskirts of Colombo. After getting out of his car, he motioned for them to follow him. He flashed an ID to a shocked officer outside, speaking to the woman in Sinhalese. Gwen wasn't surprised at the officer's reaction, Arjun's face was still bloody and bruised and his clothing dishevelled. Nevertheless, she stepped aside to let them in.

"This way," Arjun said, turning to Gwen and Graham.

Gwen was on tenterhooks as they followed the bruised detective inside the antiquated building. Once inside, however, there was nothing old about the flashy new computers on the desks in the main briefing room. An enormous man with an equally enormous girth emerged from the office. He had a huge smile on his face, which quickly turned into a concerned frown when he saw the state of Arjun. He spoke roughly in Sinhalese to an officer who scurried off to do whatever he'd been told. Arjun and the man had a brief conversation before Arjun turned to Gwen and Graham, speaking in English.

"In here." He motioned to his friend's office.

Once they were seated, Arjun introduced them to the officer. "This is my brother-in-law, Remi. These are my new friends, Dr Graham Bentley and Gwen Sumner."

The man named Remi peered at them through thick-lensed spectacles before shaking their hands. "Arjun told me you rescued him from an evil fate. I can't thank you enough." He spoke with a heavy accent, just distinguishable as English.

Before they could reply, the officer who had been sent on an errand entered the office carrying a tray of hot drinks. Remi waved him away, and the man left, closing the door behind him.

Arjun took his drink, waving away Remi's offer to look at his face. He turned to Gwen and Graham. "Excuse me, my brother-in-law speaks a little English, but not a lot, so I'm going to have to explain in Sinhalese."

After helping themselves to mugs of tea from the

tray, they waited for Arjun to finish. Gwen sipped the welcome drink while watching the interactions between the two men. At first, it was friendly, even jocular, but soon Remi's face turned more serious. He was about ten years older than Arjun, Gwen guessed, and sported a beard and moustache. His head was as large as the rest of him, almost concealing his short neck. As Gwen watched him tense, she feared the many bulges were going to burst his shirt, revealing something like the Incredible Hulk, they tightened so much. Remi fired multiple questions at Arjun, shaking his head and muttering what could be expletives from the tone.

Once Arjun stopped speaking, Remi picked up the phone on his desk, speaking in short, sharp sentences to whoever was on the other end of the line. When he put the phone down, he sat back, grinning. His chair groaned in complaint.

Arjun explained. "Remi's aunt works for the Bribery Commission. She's sending someone over to get into the files on that disk you have."

Remi was on the phone again.

"Now he's calling his father."

"Who also happens to be high up the food chain," said Gwen, grinning.

"You could say that. He's the Inspector General of

Police – our highest authority, although he answers to the government. I would have involved them after doing some more digging. I'm sure you understand I had to tread carefully and confirm that what you were telling me was true. But after tonight, it's imperative we put a stop to de Silva's corruption. We still need evidence, though. Without it, de Silva can deny any involvement. I'm sure he's got a plan that, once he finds out you sent his goons away and I've escaped, he'll set in motion."

"What can we do to help?" Gwen asked.

"We need to slow de Silva down. I have a plan, but it's a dangerous one. Remi doesn't like it."

Graham's brow furrowed as Arjun explained what he had in mind. "Can't we just wait and see what's on the stick?"

"Every minute we hesitate gives de Silva time to implement his backup plan. Plus, we don't know how many people in the central station are involved. I can take a guess, but we need to call them out. We might already be too late."

Graham sighed heavily, but Gwen was determined not to let this man get away with murder. "I'll do it. He already suspects me because he saw me at the hospital, and I'm Australian. It will sound better coming from me."

"What makes you think he'll believe a word you say?" Graham asked.

"My desperation to see Tiffany blameless is genuine enough. I'll be as convincing as I can be."

"You realise he'll kill you in an instant if he suspects you're lying?" Arjun said, warning in his eyes.

"He could kill us anyway," said Graham.

"Us?"

"We started this together. We'll finish it together."

"As I said previously, de Silva is a cautious man. He'll want to know what you have before he does anything drastic. I'm certain he'll at least hear you out."

"In that case, we should get on with it before I change my mind," said Gwen.

At that moment, Remi put the phone down and looked up at Arjun, speaking rapidly once more. Arjun's face clouded over.

"We need to leave at once. I'm a wanted man. It appears de Silva has played a different hand. It's me who's wanted for murder and corruption. There's a 'shoot on sight' order out for me."

Gwen felt her heart pounding. "What do we do now?"

"Similar to what we were going to do." Arjun

spoke to Remi, who opened a desk drawer and handed him a phone. Remi remonstrated with Arjun.

"What?" Graham asked.

"He wants me to lie low until they've uncovered what's on your memory stick."

"He has a point," said Graham.

"I can't risk it. de Silva's too clever. The only way to get him is to draw him out."

Arjun had another heated conversation with Remi, ending with the man standing up and shaking his hand. "He'll do what he can. Please leave the memory stick here."

Graham hesitated momentarily. Gwen knew he was weighing whether to trust Arjun's brother-in-law, but they had little choice. He handed it over.

"We'll take your car. Remi will hide mine in a place he knows. No-one here will give us away, and if they do, all he'll know is that we came here and Remi chucked us out. Follow my lead."

Right on cue, Remi started shouting at Arjun, ushering him to the door. Arjun yelled back, storming out of the station and heading onto the street with Gwen and Graham in hot pursuit. Remi was still following and bellowing when they got into the car.

"Take a left and go round the back," said Arjun.

Gwen did as instructed, turning into a narrow lane that led to a steel-fenced car park.

"Stop." Gwen braked. "Wait here." Arjun got out of the car and slid into a side gate, keeping to the periphery as he moved.

"He's avoiding the cameras," said Graham, pointing upwards. The car, too, was out of view of where the cameras were pointing.

Arjun came back moments later, accompanied by a uniformed officer holding a first-aid kit in her hands, while he carried what looked like a gun case. He also holstered a handgun, replacing the one de Silva's goons had taken from him earlier.

"This is Chalitha."

"Charlie. Everyone calls me Charlie," the young woman said.

Arjun and Charlie climbed into the back seat, and she opened the first-aid kit, dabbing at his face. "She studied at Cambridge. She'll go far," said Arjun with a chuckle.

"Good to meet you," said Gwen.

"Another member of the family?" Graham asked.

"Remi's niece. Now, reverse and take a right, then head back to the warehouse. Chalitha can practise her first aid skills on the way."

Charlie frowned, but Gwen wasn't sure whether it was because he insisted on calling her Chalitha or whether it was the challenge of trying to dress wounds inside a moving vehicle. Gwen sympathised.

Gwen's stomach was doing somersaults. Focusing on the road was the only thing that kept her from giving way to the fear building up inside.

24

Gwen steeled herself before tapping the number Arjun had given her. He answered after a few rings.

"Detective Inspector de Silva," he snapped.

"This is Gwen Sumner from the *Coral Queen*. We met the other day." Gwen hoped he wouldn't detect the tremor in her voice.

"Yes. I remember. The Australian who doesn't know anyone working at the hospital. What can I do for you?"

Gwen inhaled and exhaled before saying, "It's what I can do for you, Inspector."

"Just a minute." Gwen heard voices receding into the background, suggesting de Silva was moving away from prying ears.

"What's this about?"

"I know who you are and what you did. There's evidence."

"I don't know what you're talking about, Sister Sumner, and I'm a busy man, so I suggest you get to the point."

"You murdered Davi Ranasinghe and threatened my cousin Tiffany Lee. I have proof, but for my cousin's sake, I'm willing to cut a deal."

"That's a serious accusation. If you have evidence of a crime, I suggest you hand it over to the police." He was being cautious, as Arjun had suggested he would be. They were recording the conversation, and de Silva was clever enough not to fall for plan A.

Plan B it was then. "Okay. If you don't want to make a deal, why don't we meet at the station, and I'll hand it over there?"

After a brief hesitation, he said, "Why don't you do that... Oh, hang on... Sorry about that. I've been called out. Tell me where you are, and as soon as I've finished, I'll meet you."

Gwen raised a questioning eyebrow at Arjun, who was listening in. He nodded. "I also know where your missing detective is."

"Then you need to tell me. He's wanted for the murder you're accusing me of. The man is armed and dangerous, Sister Sumner. I don't know what you think you know, but you're putting yourself in grave danger."

He was right about that, but not from Arjun. Gwen exhaled. "I'm sure you've traced the call by now. I'll see you when you get here."

"Is Dr Bentley with you?"

"The doctor knows nothing about this. He's back on board the *Coral Queen*." Gwen ended the call.

"He's on his way."

Graham exhaled, as though he'd been holding his breath the whole time. "This is madness. He won't come alone."

"Time for you two to leave," said Arjun. "Give me your phone." He looked at Gwen.

"We can't leave you here alone," she said.

"You have to. Chalitha will accompany you back to your ship, and whatever happens, don't return here." Arjun said something to Charlie in Sinhalese, most likely reinforcing his order.

Gwen opened her mouth to protest, but Graham took her arm. "Arjun's right. We don't stand a chance in a firefight. He does."

"Listen to him," said Arjun. "You have about fifteen minutes before they get here."

Gwen handed over her phone, tears stinging the back of her eyes. She looked around the industrial estate that had become familiar over the past few days. There were plenty of places Arjun could take cover, but it was the dead of night, and no-one would hear if things went wrong. de Silva wouldn't be alone when he came. His corrupt cronies and maybe a few hired hands would be with him. Arjun was either exceptionally brave or totally foolish.

Graham took her arm. "Come on."

Gwen's legs felt like lead, and her mind conflicted as she followed Graham. He opened the door and ushered her into the passenger seat. Charlie sat in the back, saying nothing. She, too, looked worried. By the time Graham started the engine, Arjun was already heading towards the warehouse with the case he'd picked up from Remi. Gwen hoped it would be enough.

"Good luck, Arjun," Graham muttered as he drove away, tyres screeching as he picked up speed.

"If I'd realised he was going to send us away, I never would have agreed to that," said Gwen.

"Which is why he didn't mention it," said Graham.

"You're being very pragmatic about this. That man is risking his life for us," said Gwen.

"It's his job," said Graham.

Gwen felt a sudden surge of anger. "Is that all you've got to say? We're medics, for goodness' sake."

"I can't let anything happen to you, Gwen."

Graham's voice was thick with emotion. She heard him swallow hard, realising leaving Arjun was just as difficult for him as it was for her.

"What about you? Are you prepared to leave without trying to help?" Gwen turned to look at Charlie in the back.

Charlie was biting her bottom lip. "I don't have any choice."

"Does your Uncle Remi know what Arjun's planning?"

Charlie didn't answer, instead staring at her hands.

"The more I think about their disagreement and that charade back at the station, the more I believe they have a plan. They are setting a trap that, hopefully, de Silva will fall right into," said Graham.

"In that case, turn the car around. I want to see that man get his comeuppance."

"What if I'm wrong and he's doing this alone?"

"Then we'll die doing the right thing. We just can't leave him."

"What do you think?" Graham checked with Charlie through the rear-view mirror.

"If I know my uncle, he'll have a plan to help, but—"

"But what?" Gwen snapped.

"He would need permission. I was just told to

meet Arjun at the back of the station. If they are going to do something, I don't know what it is."

"We should still turn back. Arjun has already been beaten to a pulp. He might not be thinking straight," said Gwen.

"He looked in a bad way," said Charlie.

Graham turned his head to look at Gwen as he reduced speed. "You can be really stubborn sometimes, Sister Sumner."

Gwen grinned. "Let's hope your theory is right, and Remi brings the cavalry, or my stubbornness might just get us all killed." Gwen sighed. *And we'll never get the chance to see where our relationship might go*, went unsaid.

25

Graham didn't drive into the industrial estate. Charlie instructed him to take a left turn and drive along a dirt track, which he presumed led to a farm. There was no lighting other than that from the car's headlights. Hills on either side of the track provided cover. About half a mile along, Charlie spoke.

"Pull in here."

Graham pulled over to the left side of the track onto a verge and cut the engine.

"We'll walk from here," said Charlie. Having decided to go against instructions, Graham felt confident she would ensure their safety if she could.

Gwen put her hand on the door handle, but he grasped her arm. She turned to look at him. "We have to do what Arjun and Charlie say and stay out of harm's way. That means staying out of sight, no matter what happens."

Her eyes glinting in the moonlight betrayed her inner struggle. "Fine."

The three of them walked in silence until they heard tyres screeching to a stop a short distance away. Reaching the brow of a hill overlooking the warehouse, Charlie dropped to the ground, urging Graham and Gwen to do the same.

Four cars had stopped two hundred yards from the warehouse, their headlights trained on the building. The driver and passenger doors of each car opened simultaneously, and armed police stepped out, taking cover behind each door. When nothing happened, de Silva emerged from a car parked behind the others. He called out, "Sister Sumner, please come out."

Graham heard Arjun's voice coming from his office off to the side, speaking in Sinhalese.

Charlie withdrew her gun from her holster and pointed it down while interpreting.

"There's no-one here but me, and I'm unarmed, so you can put your guns away."

"Come out with your hands in the air, and we'll think about it," de Silva yelled.

Arjun opened the door slowly and stepped into the light from the vehicles' beams.

Graham felt Gwen stiffen next to him. Her gasp was audible. He put his finger to his lips. Charlie remained still, her gun aimed downwards.

"Remember, I'm unarmed. Tell your men not to shoot," Arjun called.

Graham could see at least eight weapons aimed at Arjun.

de Silva said something to the men before strolling closer to his target. Graham couldn't see it, but he could imagine the smarmy grin on the detective's face.

"He'll need to know where you are and where the evidence you said you had is," whispered Graham, hoping he was right.

When de Silva got closer to Arjun, a conversation took place that they could just about hear. Charlie continued her hushed interpretation. "Where is she?" de Silva barked.

"Who?" Arjun replied.

"The sister, and I bet her doctor friend is with her. We believe they are accomplices in your murder of a pharmacist."

Arjun laughed. "You really think you've got away with it, don't you?"

de Silva pointed his gun at Arjun's chest. "Where are they?"

"Safe," said Arjun. "But don't worry; so is the evidence." Arjun ignored the gun at his chest and looked over de Silva's shoulder, calling out to his men. "Are you really going to continue following this criminal? Did you know you were signing up for murder when you agreed to take a cut of his illegal dealings? And now, are you going to stand by and watch him shoot an unarmed police officer in front of you? Because if you are, you're all going down with him."

"Shut up!" de Silva snapped. "You don't have to die. Just tell me where the medics are and what the evidence is, and then you're free to go. I'll make sure your name is cleared."

"First, you tell me why you killed an innocent pharmacist and threatened a hospital nurse who's caring for the sick in our country. Do they all know it was you who killed Davi Ranasinghe?" Graham noticed a few of the officers lowering their weapons, confused. Two of them maintained their stance, weapons pointed at Arjun.

"I'm warning you, Arjun. Shut your big mouth."

"Not until you've answered my question."

"Is he telling the truth?" One officer holstered his

weapon, looking around at his colleagues. "Because he's right; I will not be a party to murder."

de Silva turned to glare at his backup. "We do what we have to do. All of you are happy to take your cut, so don't start growing a conscience on me now."

The man who had spoken removed his gun again, but this time he pointed it at de Silva. "We're not killing him." A few of the others followed his lead, but three didn't.

"This is what you call a Mexican standoff," said Arjun. "It's over, de Silva. Give it up."

de Silva turned to his men. "This detective and his newfound friends are going to put us down. We have no choice." His argument was creating confusion, so de Silva continued. "The pharmacist threatened to go to the hospital board. He wouldn't help us with the supplies we needed for our big deal. The deal that will help us all retire and live in comfort. It was for you and your families. Remember that."

Arjun spoke loudly. "So why did you execute the man in front of the foreign nurse? What had she done to deserve that?"

de Silva continued speaking to his men. "She was the pharmacist's friend. The best way to keep her quiet was to scare her and use her so that she has no comeback."

"So, you shot the man dead in her condo,

traumatising her for life. That's who this man you follow is. You're fools listening to him."

"I've heard enough," said the man who had spoken up. He and his friend holstered their weapons and got back inside their vehicle.

Satisfied that his own men would not shoot him, de Silva turned to Arjun and held his gun to his chest again. "So have I. I'll find Sister Sumner, the doctor, and her cousin, and we'll put all of this behind us."

"I don't think so," said Arjun.

Suddenly, cars came pouring in from all around them, and a helicopter appeared overhead. A voice rang out through a loudspeaker. "Drop your weapons."

de Silva turned around as Remi jumped out of a car and aimed a rifle at him. "Drop it."

"What are you doing? This man's wanted for murder," de Silva protested.

Remi stepped forward. "I said drop it. Nothing would give me more pleasure than to shoot you right now." Charlie's interpreting was faster and more cheerful now.

Graham watched de Silva drop his handgun, and Remi spun him around, roughly applying handcuffs. The rest of de Silva's men were being rounded into a police van.

"You've got this all wrong. We were just about to make an arrest."

"This is everything you need," said Arjun, removing a tape from his jacket pocket and a wire.

de Silva cursed. "She didn't have any evidence, did she?"

"Not enough. But we do now." Arjun looked at Remi. "Did you find what was on the disk?"

"Enough to put Mrs Mendis away for a long time. You were right though, the records didn't name corrupt officers. My father is delighted with your work."

"Who?" de Silva grunted.

"He's the Chief of Police, and I don't think he's very happy with you. The Bribery and Corruption Office has been informed, and your little scheme ends right now.

Every officer you work with will be under investigation until we've weeded out this corruption," said Remi. "Well done, Arjun. And thank you."

Graham and Charlie had been so engrossed in what was going on below that they hadn't realised Gwen had left their hiding place. They leapt up and hurried to join her, all shaking Arjun's hands.

"I thought I told you to go back to the ship." He glared at Charlie.

"Don't blame her. We couldn't resist seeing this guy arrested," said Gwen.

de Silva's face revealed hatred and fear, but most of all, fear. Two officers arrived to take him away. Remi grinned at them, patting his niece on the back.

"She was always a rebel. You worked out our plan, then?"

"We weren't sure but hoped there was one," said Graham. "Charlie would have kept us safe."

"Of that, I have no doubt," said Remi, grinning.

"We'll need the name of that porter you mentioned," said Arjun. "His testimony, along with the evidence we already have, will ensure these so-called officers and Mrs Mendis get what's coming to them."

Gwen wrote down Sim's name in the notebook Arjun handed her before saying, "Thank you so much, Arjun. All of you," she added, "but it's time for us to go. I need to call Tiff." Gwen reached into her handbag and handed him a sheet of paper. "She wrote down what happened that morning and described the two men who entered her flat."

"Thank you. Tell Tiffany it's safe for her to return to Colombo, and that we can confirm this statement when she's ready." He pocketed the sheet of paper.

Graham noticed the light in Arjun's eyes as he

mentioned Tiffany's name. He wondered if others could see the same in his when he was with Gwen.

26

Gwen's heart fluttered with a mix of relief and apprehension as she stood outside Nalini Bandara's house. She glanced at Graham, her unexpected partner in a horrendous situation. Unresolved feelings hung between them like the humid air surrounding the lush gardens of the estate.

"Ready?" Graham asked, his eyes filled with relief and empathy.

Gwen nodded, her fingers curling around the handle of her bag. "You bet."

Graham pressed the doorbell, sending a chime echoing through the house. A moment later, the door swung open, and Nalini's welcoming smile greeted them.

Before she could say anything, Tiffany rushed to the door, pulling Gwen into an embrace. "It's so good to see you, Gwen."

"Welcome back," said Nalini, inviting them inside.

Gwen and Tiffany locked arms; Gwen noticed the amused grin on Graham's face as he followed.

"Thank you, Mrs Bandara," she said.

"You should know by now to call me Nalini," the older woman insisted, leading them to her sitting room. "We are so glad you are both safe."

As they followed Nalini into the spacious sitting room filled with comfortable furniture and shelves lined with books, Gwen felt the tension of the past four days ease.

"Please, have a seat," Nalini gestured to the plush armchairs, her gaze flickering between Gwen and Graham with a look that was difficult to interpret. "I'll get us some tea and refreshments."

"Let me," said Tiffany, heading to the kitchen.

Gwen followed her cousin, and once the tea was brewed, she and Tiff settled on a sofa while Graham chose an armchair next to her, and Nalini took the other.

Gwen's hands trembled as she poured tea into the cups.

"Are you all right?" Graham asked, his voice low and concerned.

Gwen forced a smile. "I think it's the adrenaline release."

"Understandable," he said, reaching out to give her hand a quick squeeze. "I feel the same."

Gwen looked at their entwined fingers and was struck by the warmth of his touch. Her heart skipped a beat as she realised how much she had come to rely on him during this ordeal. But there were still so many unanswered questions and unspoken fears.

"I hope you enjoy the tea. It's a special blend from my garden," said Nalini.

"It's wonderful. Thank you," Graham said after releasing Gwen's hand and taking a sip.

"Okay. I can't wait any longer," said Tiffany. "Tell me what happened."

As Gwen and Graham recounted the story from their first visit to the hospital to their sneaking into Priya Mendis's office and Arjun's involvement, Gwen said, "Good call, by the way; he was marvellous." She saw the same light in her cousin's eyes as she had in Arjun's.

"And very brave," added Graham. "Without him, it wouldn't have been possible."

Gwen skimmed over how Arjun had been beaten and then set a trap, putting his life at risk, which led to de Silva's arrest. Gwen took a deep breath as she finished the story, her fingers curled around the warm porcelain teacup. The steam tickled her nose along with the scent of bergamot and lemongrass.

"This is wonderful news!" Nalini exclaimed, relief flooding her features. "I was afraid Tiffany here would take matters into her own hands."

Graham nodded, his eyes serious. "You're safe to go back to work if you want to. I think you'll find a friend in Elize too."

"The head of pharmacy? Davi spoke highly of her."

"She'll be pleased to know of his innocence; she's been helpful," said Gwen.

"I'll make a point of getting to know her better," said Tiffany.

"And, as well as giving your statement to the police, I think you might get a dinner invitation when you return to Colombo," Gwen added with a grin.

Tiffany flushed but didn't comment. Instead, she looked at Nalini. "Your kindness and support have meant more than you know. I don't know how I will ever repay you."

"Hear, hear," said Graham.

"It was nothing," said Nalini. "I shall miss you, but not the worry about what might happen if you were ever discovered."

Tears surfaced in Tiffany's eyes. "You never let on."

"That wouldn't have been helpful." Nalini patted Tiffany's hand.

"Thank you... all of you," Tiffany said, her voice quivering. "I don't know how I can ever repay any of you, to be honest."

"Seeing you safe is all the repayment we need," Gwen said. "Plus, a few days' holiday might be nice."

They all laughed.

"That, I can promise you," said Tiffany.

With tea finished, Tiffany excused herself to pack a few last things before they left.

Nalini studied Gwen and Graham, setting her teacup down and clearing her throat. "If I may be so bold, I'd like to share a story with you. It's about heartache and finding love again when one least expects it."

Gwen's eyes met their host's as she began.

"After my beloved husband, Graham's friend, died, the pain was unbearable, and for a long time, I believed I would never find happiness again. I know you've felt that way since your wife died; Ramesh told me. But life has a way of surprising us." Nalini paused. "About six months ago, I met someone who has changed all that. He showed me it's possible to open your heart again, even after suffering such a significant loss. It doesn't mean I've stopped loving

Ramesh, but he wouldn't have wanted me to live my life in a permanent state of grief."

Gwen felt uncomfortable as her heart fluttered, sensing Nalini's words were meant for her and Graham. Her mind was conflicted, doubting either of them could find the courage to face the fear of suffering heartbreak again.

"Sometimes," Nalini continued, her gaze fixed on Gwen and Graham, "all it takes is a leap of faith and the willingness to trust that life can offer us second chances." Her words lingered until she stood up. "And now, I must spend a little time with Tiffany before she leaves."

As Nalini left the room, her words settled over them, and silence enveloped the space.

Graham's eyes locked onto Gwen's, and in that moment, she knew they could no longer ignore the unspoken feelings that had been simmering between them for days, if not months. The surrounding air seemed to crackle with possibility, both thrilling and daunting.

"Listen, Gwen," Graham began, his voice trembling slightly. "I've been through a lot in my life. I lost the woman I loved, and it hurt more than I had ever imagined. Since then, I've tried to protect myself by not getting emotionally involved again." His hands trembled. "But since I met you, I can't deny things have changed. You've made me feel things I haven't felt for a very long time."

Gwen's chest swelled with emotion; her eyes locked on his. They were filled with a tender intensity that made it difficult for her to speak. "Graham, I—"

"Please, let me finish," he interrupted, his voice tremulous. "Or I might never get to say this. I'm scared, Gwen. I'm scared of losing someone again. But I'm also scared of missing out on this chance at happiness because I'm too afraid to take a risk." He paused, swallowing hard. "I guess what I'm trying to say is... I think... I know... I've fallen in love with you. And I don't know what that means for our future, but I'd like to find out."

As Graham's confession hung in the air, Gwen felt a mixture of relief and vulnerability wash over her. He had bared his soul. What was she going to do about it?

Graham stared at her, his eyes searching, as if trying to make sense of this sudden upheaval in their relationship. Then, slowly, she reached across the space between them and took his hands in her own.

"I won't pretend I have the answers you need, or that I know what's going to happen next, but I know one thing: I feel the same way about you."

Gwen's breath caught in her throat as she registered the words spilling from her mouth. They were at a crossroads, facing an unknown future, but having spent the last few days with this tender and caring man, it no longer seemed quite so terrifying.

Graham's eyes bore into hers as he squeezed her hands. "I'm sorry for being such a coward. I've been hesitant because of my past. When I lost my wife, I thought that was it for me – I wouldn't find love again, and it almost felt disloyal to feel about you the way I do. Nalini's right on that score."

"And now?" Gwen's heart ached for him. She searched his eyes.

"My kids have always told me their mother would want me to find happiness. I've been stubborn about it, but now I realise they've been right all along. If you're willing, I'd be grateful for the chance to explore these feelings with you, Gwen."

"My failed relationships haven't left me with much hope," she confessed. "But with you, it's different. If you're willing, then so am I."

"We'll face our fears, one at a time." Graham moved to sit next to her, and as their eyes met, he took her in his arms and kissed her tenderly.

When he released her, they shared a moment of silent intimacy. The path ahead was uncertain and possibly fraught with heartache, but the possibility of love – of finding happiness together – was a risk worth taking.

Gwen broke the silence. "Come on, mate. Time to get my cousin home. I'm looking forward to a holiday."

Graham smiled warmly. "Who would have thought an escape in Sri Lanka would be so thrilling?"

"And life-changing," said Gwen. Her heart was ready to burst with happiness. "There's one condition, though."

"Conditions already?" Graham's eyes twinkled. Now, she could read them.

"We keep it quiet from the team for a bit. When Bernard hears about this, he's going to drive us both crazy."

"That's a condition I can live with, although we're going to have to tell them about our adventure. Bernard has been giving me funny looks every time I go back on board."

"We'll never hear the end of it, but at least his concentration will be on that, rather than on us."

"I have a condition of my own," said Graham.

"Oh?"

"You have to take me to that rooftop restaurant and cocktail bar you spoke so highly of."

"That would be my pleasure. We could even make

it a double date with Tiff and Arjun." Gwen felt her heart might burst with joy.

Graham stood, grinning, and held out his hand for her. She took it.

THE END

THANK YOU

If you have enjoyed reading this book, **please leave an honest review on Amazon and/or any other platform that you may use.** I read all reviews and love it when someone likes my work – it makes my day!

OTHER BOOKS BY DAWN BROOKES

Rachel Prince Mysteries

A Cruise to Murder #1

Deadly Cruise #2

Killer Cruise #3

Dying to Cruise #4

A Christmas Cruise Murder #5

Murderous Cruise Habit #6

Honeymoon Cruise Murder #7

A Murder Mystery Cruise #8

Hazardous Cruise #9

Captain's Dinner Cruise Murder #10

Corporate Cruise Murder #11

Treacherous Cruise Flirtation #12

Toxic Cruise Cocktail #13

Cruise into Darkness #14

Carlos Jacobi PI

Body in the Woods #1

The Bradgate Park Murders #2

The Museum Murders #3

Lady Marjorie Snellthorpe Mysteries

Death of a Blogger (prequel novella)

Murder at the Opera House #1

Murder in the Highlands #2

Murder at the Christmas Market #3

Murder at a Wimbledon Mansion #4

Murder in a Care Home #5

Murder at the Regatta #6

Memoirs

Hurry up Nurse: Memoirs of nurse training in the 1970s

Hurry up Nurse 2: London calling

Hurry up Nurse 3: More adventures in the life of a student nurse

BOOKS FOR CHILDREN

Ava & Oliver's Bonfire Night Adventure
Ava & Oliver's Christmas Nativity Adventure
Danny the Caterpillar
Gerry the One-Eared Cat
Suki Seal and the Plastic Ring

ABOUT THE AUTHOR

Dawn Brookes is an award winning, bestselling author of cosy mysteries and crime fiction. The *Rachel Prince Mystery* series combines a unique blend of murder, cruising and medicine with a touch of romance. The Lady Marjorie Snellthorpe mysteries sees four octogenarian friends solving murder and is packed with humour. Carlos Jacobi PI is a little grittier but Dawn remains true to her view that good fiction can still be written without cursing, graphic violence and explicit sexual content.

Dawn holds an MA in Creative Writing with Distinction and has a 39-year nursing pedigree. She loves to travel and takes regular cruise holidays, which she says are for research purposes! She brings these passions and a love of clean crime to her writing.

The surname of her Rachel Prince protagonist is in

honour of her childhood dog, Prince, who used to put his head on her knee while she lost herself in books.

Dawn also wrote a series of nursing memoirs: *Hurry up Nurse: memoirs of nurse training in the 1970s, Hurry up Nurse 2: London calling* and *Hurry up Nurse 3 More adventures in the life of a student nurse.* She worked as a hospital nurse, midwife, district nurse and community matron across her career. Before turning her hand to writing for a living, she had multiple articles published in professional journals and co-edited a nursing textbook.

Dawn grew up in Leicester, later moved to London and Berkshire, but now lives in Derbyshire. Dawn holds a Bachelor's degree with Honours and a Master's degree in education. Writing across genres, she also writes for children. Dawn has a passion for nature and loves animals, especially dogs. Animals will continue to feature in her children's books, as she believes caring for animals and nature helps children to become kinder human beings.

Printed in Dunstable, United Kingdom

78052214R00143